ELIANA-WHO-SEES-US

Eliana-Who-Sees-Us

Amani Jesu

Janesville Publishing LLC

Janesville Publishing LLC
Houston,, Texas
Visit us at www.janesvillepublishing.com

First Printing, 2022

ISBN: 978-1-958278-02-4 (pbk)
ISBN: 978-1-958278-01-7 (hb)
ISBN: 978-1-958278-00-0 (eBook)

Library of Congress Control Number: 2022910562

Cover design by: Wendy Wheeler

To Ranjan, the love of my life.

Contents

1

Worst Thanksgiving Ever

I couldn't hide in my room anymore, but I could at least cut the carrots badly.

One could argue that carrots can only be cut, and there is no good or bad—unless you're in my mom's kitchen. Mom had been working on the holiday dinner since the day before. I wasn't much help, because I never did anything right, apparently. Even for a simple task like chopping vegetables, she would hover nearby until she could swoop in and correct me. Then she would complain that she had too much to do. After a few minutes of mutilating the carrots, she dismissed me from the cutting board to sit at the kitchen table and "keep her company."

My anxiety level was higher than usual because I had decided to announce our plan today: after working like a dog my senior year of high school and full time since then, my boyfriend Chas and I were going to move in with one of his friends, and we would both start art school in January. I still couldn't afford the whole thing myself, and needed to convince Mom to contribute what she would have paid for college.

Years ago, when Dad's sudden departure made her the main breadwinner, she became a successful manager at her company. Unfortunately, she never let us forget it. She took care of us, but she also kept a mental ledger of every favor, every slight. My brother, Rob, was still in the debt column for a DUI court case from a year ago.

"Put the baby carrots in a dish on the high chair," she said over her shoulder. She was excited that Rob and his family were coming for dinner. Their toddler had just started walking. The high chair was more of a baby containment device than a chair.

However, three o'clock came and went, the food was ready, and they hadn't arrived yet. They never had been on time before, but she was fretting and complaining about it. After a few snippy texts to Chas to blow off steam, he stopped responding. But if Chas had at least been on time, it would have taken the tension down a notch, and I was getting annoyed. Maybe he wasn't responding because he was driving over.

I tried to make things better with Mom by suggesting we watch a movie, shuffling a deck of cards enticingly, and even picking up the phone to call and check on Rob's progress, but she wasn't having any of it. Eventually, I settled into my favorite spot on the sofa, at the far end where I could get a view of the street out the window—a view of freedom—and put on *It's a Wonderful Life.* The idea was to lure Mom in so she would sit and watch it with me, but she only came in the room to look out the window any time she heard a voice or car door outside.

The cozy familiarity of George Bailey and his small town helped me relax. I used to hate that movie; to me, it was about a guy who wants to leave and keeps getting held back by the whiny, non-adventurous people in his life who couldn't take care of themselves. But I finally saw it as a choice—George Bailey's choice to stay and be with people he cared about.

However, it is a little hard to follow a movie when someone is sighing behind you.

"Tina probably didn't start the casserole early enough. I bet it's still in the oven."

"Good," I said without taking my eyes off the TV, "then we won't have to take time to reheat it."

After about ninety minutes, Rob showed up. I left the movie on to give the appearance we weren't waiting to jump on him like unfed dogs as soon as he walked in. When Mom moved away from the window, I could see Tina carrying my half-asleep nephew. They walked toward the porch slowly, almost like they weren't eager to be there.

Mom opened the door and waved them in. Houston weather can be chilly or balmy on Thanksgiving. This year it picked moody with cloudy skies, but it was warm enough that a fly buzzed in the door.

"I was worried something happened to you."

"Mom, I'm sorry we're late. We did the best we could. Bobby had an upset tummy."

Instead of welcoming them in, she stood with her hands clasped, like she wasn't ready to let it go. Tina put little Bobby on the floor, and he clung to her leg with one arm. He looked at Mom and thrust his plush dinosaur at her, breaking the tension.

"Hey, Sis," Rob gave me a quick hug while balancing a casserole in the other arm. "Where's your boyfriend?"

"He must be on his way. I'll give him a call." I used the opportunity to escape to my bedroom while they settled in, shutting the door as I heard Mom say, "I hope the food isn't all overcooked now . . ."

Chas picked up on the first ring. "Hello . . . oh . . . El." Not a good start.

"Hey, Chas. Rob and Tina just walked in, so we haven't started eating yet, but, uh, are you almost here?" I knew he wasn't, because kitchen noises clattered in the background. A door closed and muted the sounds.

"El, sorry." He drew a breath in slowly, and I held mine. "My aunt came down from Chicago for Thanksgiving dinner, and there's a lot of stuff going on."

"What stuff?" I was getting angry. "Chas, we planned this. I wanted to tell Mom about the apartment and everything with you here."

"I wanted to talk about this in person, tonight . . ." His voice was peevish now. "But since you called, I have an . . . opportunity."

I waited and heard muffled crunching. Was he eating while he talked to me? The hell, man! My stomach rumbled.

"My aunt said I can stay with her in Chicago and go to school there. I'm going to go back with her when she goes home."

"To . . . uh, look for an apartment?" He was silent. Not even chewing. Was he leaving me? Seriously? "Chas, I'm coming to your house. We have to talk. Now." I bent for my purse, but all my closet cleaning had cluttered my bedroom floor. I tripped over a pile marked for donations and found it.

"No, El, all my family is still here, and look, I . . . I'll see you at Mariah's. Are you still going there after dinner?"

"*My* plans haven't changed!"

I hung up without saying goodbye. The nerve! Piles of clothes, books, and beauty items that were the sum of my material possessions surrounded me. Chas had seemed too calm recently about packing his stuff, waving it off as something that could wait. Come to think of it, we hadn't visited Gary, our future roommate, in some time either.

Cool water splashed on my face helped me focus. Dinner and cleanup couldn't take more than an hour and a half. Then I would see him at Mariah's and talk this out. If he wanted both of us to go to Chicago, we would find a way. Judging by his voice, it was a slim hope, but I tried to hold on to it. Feeling lighter, I went to the kitchen.

Five minutes later, at the dinner table, Mom and Rob were trying to out-martyr each other while I sat, waiting for it to be over, the dry turkey on the platter in front of me growing cold.

"I didn't want to call because I know how you get . . ." Mom said.

"How do I get, Mom?"

She opened her mouth to speak, then just sighed and waved her hand weakly. "You get all uptight at me."

His mouth thinned from tight to lipless. "I never said we would be here at a certain time. I am very careful not to give a certain time, because I know how *you* get."

Mom went back to the sink to busy herself with things that were supposedly done hours ago. She ran out of things to fuss with and stood at the sink, wiping her face while keeping it hidden.

We waited awkwardly until Mom finally sat down with us, gave the blessing, and started passing around food. Her silence was loud.

"Tina, the casserole looks good," I said. She seemed surprised, and I looked at it again. It was green bean casserole, which I hate, and it was from the deli, not homemade. It just wasn't my day.

"They were out of the broccoli," she said apologetically.

Rob put a large serving of the green bean casserole on my plate.

"El, is this new job of yours full or part-time?"

I could already see the entire conversation unfolding, but didn't see a way to avoid it. Eating in total silence would be tense and weird. Well, more tense than it already was.

"Full-time."

"You're still not going to college? What about your plan with Chas?" He held back his smirk, but he knew we had been planning to move in together once school started. Apparently, Rob was not above throwing me under the bus to get Mom off his back.

I put down my forkful of cold turkey. "Apparently, Chas is moving to Chicago. Suddenly. Change of plans. My plans changed too." My voice wavered. "I'm going to continue to work in photography, get some experience before going to school. I'll . . . work it out." I was making this up as it came out of my mouth, but the surprise at hearing myself say it out loud kept me from crying. I tried to look unfazed. How could Chas drop me like this?

"How will you afford an apartment on minimum wage? And who's going to pay for art school?"

Mom found her voice again. "I'm not paying for art school. It's college or nothing."

"I know, Mom."

"Why would El need to pay for an apartment?" I kept my head down as she waited for his answer.

Rob was enjoying himself. We usually got along better than this. He was apparently sick of being the center of attention, but I didn't want the spotlight either. Mom's face showed she was reevaluating all my closet cleaning and organizing, plus the extra hours at work as I transitioned to my new job. "Are you moving out? Not with that actor?"

"Mom, you know his name." Eating the green beans just to be polite would be pointless, so I shoved them aside and took a bite of mashed potatoes, willing the tears not to come. Everyone was against me, but I hadn't done anything wrong. I hissed at Rob, "I said I'll work it out. It's not your problem."

"It is, if Mom has to bail you out of trouble six months from now."

"Why," I spat the words out, "because then she'll have less money to bail you out when you screw up?"

His face went pale, then brick red. I'd never seen him so mad.

"Shut up, El!" he shouted. "You're not the baby anymore."

Furious, I stood up and screamed back, "I will not shut up! I will not shut up!"

Mom lurched out of her chair and faked a faint. Badly. People who faint usually don't hold on to something and look around at everyone in the room first. Or check for furniture partway down. I guess she deserves points for risking a broken hip. Once I was sure she was actually okay and Tina was helping her back into her chair, I stormed off to my room.

It wasn't that nobody understood what I was going through; it was that nobody cared. I had to get out of there before my head exploded. Also, I had to do damage control with Chas. He couldn't just dump me over the phone.

I grabbed a gym bag and stuffed in some essentials for an overnight stay—Mariah wouldn't mind. Jeans, underwear, jammies, secret stash of Pop-Tarts, and a ragged teddy bear my dad had given me last time I saw him. I couldn't have packed so quickly even a month ago, but everything in my room was sorted into stacks with color-coded sticky notes to take, leave, or donate.

After a moment of thought, I took my stockpile of cash from its place in the back of the closet and stuffed it down into the bottom of the bag. My family was still at the dinner table, soldiering on like we hadn't had a group meltdown. Worse than after Dad left. My heart skipped a beat when I realized I was walking out like he did, but at eighteen, I was the youngest in the family; I'm not supposed to be the grown-up. I slipped out the front door as quietly as possible and drove to Mariah's on autopilot.

Chas was not the love of my life. I realized that on some level. It's not like I was "using" him to run away, though. I just thought we could both run off to an exciting future together.

The streets were practically empty; everyone must be with their families. Mariah's apartment parking lot had half the cars it normally did. A twinge of doubt hit me; was she even home from her family's house yet? With my fingers crossed, I grabbed my bag and headed for her door. I could fill her in on the details and also calm down before Chas arrived. She would help him see reason.

When I rounded the corner, I nearly ran into Chas. He was setting a note on a cardboard box on her welcome mat.

"Oh. Uh, is she not home?" I could hear music inside.

"El." He had a habit of jerking his head to flip the hair out of his eyes. He stepped forward and gripped my arms gently. I tilted my face up for a kiss, mostly out of habit; I really felt more like spitting in his face. He looked into my eyes. "There's no point discussing it further. I'm sorry I hurt you, but this is for the best. It's all in the note." He pointed toward the note like I didn't know where it was, and in one smooth motion, he patted my arm and walked past me and away.

"What?" My throat was scratchy from yelling earlier, but I couldn't keep my temper. "What makes you think . . ."

He paused and turned back. A car I hadn't noticed idling nearby honked twice. He shrugged, said, "Sorry," and trotted to the passenger side.

It was too early for it to be a Christmas gift, so I kicked the box in annoyance. At the same moment, Mariah opened the door and looked from me and my gym bag to the box.

"Are you moving in?"

I could see she was joking, but she looked horribly embarrassed when she saw my face.

"Oh, El, of course you can stay here as long as you want." She hugged me, and I felt my face scrunch up to hold the tears back. After another moment, I let them go. Mariah could never stop being the big sister. Put in a foster home at sixteen, she had grown up with a parade of younger foster siblings. She patted my back and made soothing sounds that I couldn't hear well over my sobs.

Instead of just staying one night, Mariah said she'd be glad to let me move in with her. Having a roommate would be good for her. She was working part-time as she finished her last year of college, and could use the help with rent. Considering the breakup, I preferred to pay rent to her than to Chas and his friend. Bitterly, I realized I had been saving my money to run away with a man who was running away from me. After calming down a bit, I read the note, and it set me off again.

"What? He says *I've* changed!" I read some more. "Different paths? Is this code for 'I found someone else'?" Mariah waited patiently as I paced the floor. "A little time off will give us a new perspective. I'm leaving this box with you because I can't take it with me."

That's odd; why not leave it at his parents' house? Mariah leaned forward as I yanked up the tucked-in box flap, then back again when she saw what it was.

"He returned the gifts I gave him? Who does that? What a jerk!"

She pulled the box away and pushed my cup of herbal tea toward me. "Leave it, Ellie, and don't call him again for a few days."

I lasted an entire hour before calling him, but he didn't pick up.

2

The Dumpster

Before the sun was fully up, I carried the Chas box to a restaurant a couple blocks away instead of using the apartment dumpster. Both to make sure I never accidentally saw any of it again, and to walk off some frustration. It had taken hours for me to fall asleep the night before, while every conversation we had the past week replayed in my head like it was a late night furniture store commercial.

Mariah, Chas, and I had all met in an acting class four years ago. Mariah was supplementing her budding modeling career. He thought he was star material. I was going through a phase, after horses, but before boyfriends. I should have learned to spot a lousy actor at least.

His note said something about needing to move away to wipe away last semester. Without breaking up face-to-face, I couldn't ask why I had to be wiped out too. Shifty-eyed jerk. He must have already been looking for a way to move to another city. Why didn't he just tell me? But my mental argument was pointless. Once he decided to leave, he was already gone—he just hadn't physically left.

You would think a pizza restaurant dumpster would smell better —at least a hint of yeasty goodness, but no. Breathing out more than in, I chucked in the personalized photo mug first, and it startled me with its thunderous echo. It was before dawn, and even 18th Street was quiet. If I had thrown it harder it might have broken, but it was his face I wanted to break.

His cookbook followed with a disappointing flapping noise. Should have ripped it first. He probably lied about wanting to learn to cook Indian food anyway. The hand-painted T-shirt that matched his eyes was next. I yanked at the collar to rip it. I was beginning to sweat despite the cool morning air. I finally settled for rubbing it roughly against the dumpster to dirty it and threw it in.

The photos. I squinted at them in the light of the streetlamp. I hadn't taken the time to do the traditional cigarette burn into each photo of him, which had seemed wrong to do anyway, because I took the photos. They were my art. But, art though they were, I ripped them and threw the pieces away like trash. The breeze lifted a few fragments and scattered them to the ground. I didn't pick them up.

The dumpster was still echoing hollowly when I came to my last token: the birthday card I'd made for him just a month ago. Outside was rough handmade paper, and inside, my fingers slid over the slick photo paper. The image was of the two of us in black and white except for our eyes; his were tinted golden brown, and mine green. I had heavily overexposed it to give it a fuzzy softness. I knew time would eventually make my memories of him fuzzy, but right now they were like shards of glass. I closed my eyes and tore the card; the photo. I didn't want to risk seeing a fragment of his face looking at me one last time. Eyes still shut, I tossed it in, grazing my hand on the gritty rim of the dumpster.

I walked back to the apartment parking lot. Glass or gravel crunched under my feet. Throwing it all out hadn't felt as satisfying as I thought it would. I just felt hollow, echoing like the rusting dumpster. Mariah would be up by now. She would want to know what happened and make me drink hot tea and tell her about it. Indecision gripped me, and I wavered between my car and the path to her door. I wanted sympathy, but I made myself go to my car. I would see her later at work anyway.

The car chugged out vapor clouds as it warmed up. I took my camera bag out of the trunk in time to see the local feral cat stretch and hop off a nearby car. Pulling the camera out, I settled my camera bag on the passenger side floor and dropped a tote bag of work stuff next to it. I followed the cat a few paces.

Tuxedo, a young black and white tomcat with an inquisitive nature, was playing hard to get. He paused and flicked an ear at the sound of my camera, then looked coyly over one shoulder.

The best thing I learned in acting class was that I'm not an actor —I'm a photographer. In acting, I always seemed to hold back, unable to give myself completely to the role I was playing. But one day, the teacher was giving us tips on how to look our best in audition snapshots. She handed me the camera so she could demonstrate the pose she wanted from Mariah, and I was hooked. I marveled at the tight, hard weight of the camera, like a gun, and when I looked through the viewfinder, the bulk of the room disappeared. It forced me to focus on one thing, and the framing and isolation of one thing can make you look at it like you've never seen it before. Meanwhile, Mariah, who already loved being the focal point, went into fashion spread mode. Others joined in, and the teacher had to stop the spontaneous modeling session that broke out.

Tuxedo grew bored or hungry and sauntered off. I got one last shot as he squinted his eyes at the sunrise. Sighing, I got in the car and packed the camera away.

Chas had encouraged me to go to art school with him so I could study photography, yet he always made little comments when I had the camera with me, such as saying that guys would think I was flirting if I took pictures of them or that it was going to be expensive to get started as a pro. If he thought I was paying too much attention to taking pictures, he would say he might as well not be there.

The only thing I hate more than being lied to is being manipulated. When you look through a camera, what you see is what you get.

3
─
─

The Mall

The crowd at the mall was manageable for Black Friday; it looked like our mall was becoming unpopular. Though, the salespeople still looked tense, as if prepared for the worst. I snapped some photos of people filing in through a mall entrance. I would face my own crush of customers at Snapshot during the next few weeks. Now that my training period was finished, I could start doing portrait sessions. Bored teenagers liked our props and ladder-climbing businessmen needed headshots. I was just glad to have a job that let me work with a camera. I had time before my shift started, so I decided to splurge and buy a coffee.

Kids were already camped out, waiting at the mall's Cineplex for the latest holiday blockbuster, *The Meaning of Christmas,* while their parents shopped. The coffee shop line stretched across the opposite wall. An employee I knew from Claire's Boutique let me cut in the line.

A TV crew for a local kids' show worked their way along the movie line. All of us who were not texting watched the cheerful reporter in a Santa hat and red and white over the knee socks interview people waiting for the theater to open. I found myself staring as if it were already on TV. She moved away from the movie line to zero in on a trio of teenage guys standing in the middle of the entryway. Stephanie what's-her-name's audience was the middle school crowd, but these guys looked older. The tallest—and cutest—one was maybe eighteen, my age. She snuggled in right next to him.

"What's your name?" she asked, smiling up at him.

"Shay." He seemed remarkably relaxed considering the impromptu TV interview.

"So, Shay, what do you hope Santa brings you?"

Shay said, "Cookies and milk."

She gave a surprised laugh. "Great! And what does Christmas mean to you?"

He looked uncomfortable. Seconds ticked by.

As if to hurry him along, Stephanie asked, "Is it about spending time with family or getting gifts?" She turned to the camera with a brilliant smile.

Shay said to her, "Christmas is about the Son of God coming to Earth to die for our sins to reunite us with our creator."

Stephanie looked shocked, then forced a laugh. "Okay, Shay, thanks." She walked sideways away from him, working her way to a knot of middle schoolers in the movie line. "Let's see what these guys think." The camera operator trailed along. Mall cops tensed up like they had a situation on their hands and watched the guys stroll out of the theater area. Shay and his buddies went past the coffee shop just as I got my drink. It didn't taste all that great.

I trudged toward the studio. The three guys meandered ahead of me, through the crush of shoppers, then started caroling. They didn't seem to be part of any organized entertainment for the mall. Were they drunk? It was too early to be so happy.

Why even ask people about the meaning of Christmas? Christmas is . . . well, it's the same every year.

***

Shay and his friends sang "O Come All Ye Faithful." People smiled as they walked by, and little kids pointed. I followed at a safe distance, my camera bag bumping along on my hip as I sidestepped shoppers. They reached a photo studio with a display table out front. My studio. I had been working there a grand total of three weeks, and today was payday. Christmas indeed.

Susan, our tightfisted Scrooge of a studio manager, was out of the back office and lending a hand out front. She saw the guys approaching and spoke up from behind a display table set up at the entrance. "Portrait?" Her voice sounded tired, and the day was just starting.

Shay veered over. "What was that?" he said as he smiled at her.

I slipped past them and behind the shelter of the studio's front counter.

Susan seemed shocked he had responded. Everyone else just drifted by like she was a TV commercial. But I was glad these guys didn't. Shay, with his charming smile and tousled hair, seemed interesting. *No, I don't need to get hooked on another guy already.* I sipped my disappointing coffee and grimaced.

Susan held out a flyer and pointed at the framed sample photos on the table. "Would you like a portrait for Christmas? They make great gifts." She was curt with the photographers, so I was curious whether she would strong-arm potential customers. Maybe he'd spring for the portrait, and I'd get to take it. *Come on Susan, don't blow it.*

He smoothed his hair back and straightened his coat. "Of course a photo of me would make a great gift. I'm gorgeous."

Susan stared like a fish. One of the other guys leaned in and said, "He's kidding." The other guy took the flyer from Susan and grabbed Shay's coat sleeve before yanking him backward. Shay acted abashed, but with a last charming smile and a wink, left Susan looking after him, a grin on her face at last. With a sigh, she wandered into the studio.

A customer came over to pick up photos just as Susan walked in, stretching her arms and back. I pulled up his information on the computer, hoping to give Susan no reasons to piddle around and delay my check. She bustled over and joined me behind the counter. "Eliana. How are you?" I held in a sigh; I knew she didn't want the real answer to that question.

"Hi, Susan. I'm fine." I surrendered the customer's photo envelope to her as she elbowed me out of the way.

She turned to the customer, who was holding out his credit card.

I said, "I'll be back in a minute; could you get my check?"

"Oh, sure." Susan turned toward me, leaving the customer with his hand out, his credit card floating. "You're not taking food into the studio, are you?" The customer snapped his card down onto the counter, causing her to jump. "I'm sorry, let me get that . . . how was your photo session?"

I headed for the sanctuary of the studios. The hallway opened to rooms on each side with your basic backdrops and lighting for anything from family portraits to passport photos. Deeper in, the largest room held props for more elaborate or themed portraits. An assortment of scenery lined the back wall—flowered archways, columns, fake grass carpets for Easter, even a gold-painted throne fit for the Easter Bunny. A wide area, emptied of Christmas decorations, had become an unofficial employee lounge and changing room.

The studio handled the mall's Santa photos every year. When I applied for the job, I swore I would never do Santa photo duty, even if having that additional part-time gig would get me close to forty hours per week. The photogs who did it insisted it wasn't that bad, but I was determined to leverage my freelance experience to keep me from the more mundane tasks. However, not only was I required to do Christmas photos, I was not doing them as a photographer.

I was an elf.

4

The Perfect Gift

"Eliana, daaaaahling." My favorite photo subject called to me from her perch on the golden throne. Mariah extended her lanky arms toward me as she air kissed me from across the room. "So wonderful you could come today to my palace." She was already wearing her elf costume—she had no shame. I couldn't help but be cheered up again when I saw her.

Mariah was not the stereotypical model. It was just a way to make money while she was still in school. She didn't love or hate how she looked or obsess about weight. She was fascinated with how she looked, but it was more of a ridiculous curiosity—"How do I look if I bend like this? Do I look like the letter N? What if I slant the hat like that? Does the shadow hide my eyes? Do they look scary?" She got along with people if they gave her a chance. Most were either ready to hate her or drool over her because she was a model. They didn't see past that. Mariah was one of my biggest cheerleaders in going after my dreams, and had recommended me for this job. She was one of the most down-to-earth people I had ever met, despite sitting on a golden throne at the moment.

I indicated the rumpled fake grass carpet at her feet. "Your royal bunnies seem to have escaped the palace."

Mariah looked down with exaggerated concern. "No, no dear—the royal bunnier has them out for some exercise."

I laughed for the first time that day.

"My, you have someone for your every need."

Just for fun, I put my coffee down and pulled my camera out of the bag to snap a few shots of her as "Queen Mariah." Mariah unfolded herself from the throne and sauntered, runway style, to the center of the room. "No one outranks my royal photog."

"Royal pain in the ass photog, you mean."

"Of course, that is always implied."

One last hair toss, and she looked pointedly at my tote bag. The tote bag of shame.

"Yes." I set the camera on the table. "I'll get dressed."

I dumped the tote bag's contents onto the table. I had been too grouchy last night to do a test run of the "Santa's Elf Level One" outfit after setting the box of Chas's stuff by the door for its a.m. disposal. The green tights were still in their package. The elf hat with its little bouncy tinsel antennae mocked me. I sighed and stripped down.

"Sorry Mariah, I didn't think you would be out so early, or we could have ridden together."

"That's okay. I thought you might want some time to yourself."

Mariah guarded the studio door while I changed, as there was no lock. If only she could keep me hidden the rest of the time. The synthetic blouse was cold on my skin, and the cheap green skirt fabric glittered between sewn-on felt candy canes and bells.

She smoothed out my elf vest and set the hat next to it on the table, then, puzzled, picked up two boxes of Christmas cards that I had left in the bag by mistake.

"You're going Thomas Kincaid on me? I thought cartoon reindeer were more your style?"

I grimaced. I had wanted cute, funny cards. I was trying to appear more grown-up; to show that I could stand on my own two feet. And snowy cottages are grown-up.

She peered at the back of the box. "'Wishing you a season of joy and peace.' That's kinda generic, isn't it?"

"Who analyzes Christmas card greetings? It's just stuff in script that you sign your name under."

"I like your homemade cards," Mariah said. "They're just so you."

Was she joking? She was too good a friend to be making fun of me; she knew I only made cards and gifts in the past to save money. But she couldn't have actually liked them.

With a final tug, I had the itchy green tights on and wadded up the packaging. "I'm buying stuff this year. I'm tired of doing crafts like a kid making presents for Mommy and Daddy."

"The gifts too?" Disappointment was heavy in her voice. "I loved the birdcage made out of sticks, and the doohickey you made with the links on it."

"It was a bracelet."

"Yeah, you can't get things like that in a store."

I laughed out loud. "No, you can't, because no one would pay for it!"

Mariah glanced at the cards and moved to place the elf hat on me with a few bobby pins. "Nod your head."

I did. It stayed in place with only minor discomfort. I tossed the snowy cottages back in the bag and tugged the vest on.

She seemed to be biting her tongue, but she kept her face neutral. At the mirror I added some extra blusher to make my cheeks elf-level rosy.

Mariah started placing my camera in the cushioned cutout of the hand-painted gear bag. "You don't need to do that. I can do it in a second," I said over my shoulder.

"I don't mind." Mariah had her back to me. It always took her three times longer to put the gear away than if I did it myself. She handled and examined each item as she went. She was two years older than I was—twenty to my eighteen—but people usually thought she was a lot older. I liked to tell her she had a very mature air about her, but it was the way she always kept calm and steady that gave people the impression of years of wisdom.

I shoved my clothes into the tote bag, tucked it and my jacket into a locker, and reached to Mariah for my camera bag, like always. And like always, Mariah said, "I'll do it." She slid the bag onto the locker shelf and lined it up so the scene showing mountains rising up to the clouds was in front. I closed the door, punched in a code, and we walked out into the hallway together.

My camera was my favorite possession. Last year I had a choice between getting a smart phone and my first really good camera, which was why I had a tiny flip phone. I hand-painted my camera bag in the style of a funky up-and-coming NYC handbag designer. Mariah always wanted to carry it when we did location shoots. Come to think of it, she had hinted once that I should paint another one, but she didn't need a camera bag. I realized I could get her a purse—*the* purse, the one I copied. I was relieved to have a plan, but my stomach churned a bit at the idea of buying an expensive designer item. Could I afford it? She was so laid-back that I knew she would like anything I gave her, but it had to be special. She was my best friend, and I had given her homemade crap like a little kid since we met. It would be worth it.

Click. One of the other studios was occupied. The studio owner, Jim, a middle-aged teddy bear, was putting a family of four through their paces, their holiday sweaters gleaming under the lights. "And look here," he cooed. As a unit, the four of them obeyed. *Click.*

In the lobby, a well-dressed couple sat on the couch, restraining a toddler in a reindeer outfit. I avoided making eye contact. Susan waved her hand and leaned over the counter.

"Eliana, there's a client waiting . . ." Her tone was firm, but pleasant. She couldn't be rude in front of a customer.

I grimaced, but tried to keep my voice level. "Susan, they'll have to go to Jim. I'm on elf duty today, remember?" Well, she couldn't forget, since I was in costume. I avoided looking at the couple on the couch, their daughter now leaning backward and wailing plaintively.

"Jim has someone in . . ."

I met her gaze and waited, and after a moment, she seemed to realize I wasn't going to budge and bustled to find the check. She held it out with both hands, a smile on her face. "Your first paycheck? I remember when I started here . . ."

"Yes, I'm going to buy real gifts for people this year."

As soon as I said it, I immediately regretted it. I wanted to sneak off and buy the purse without Mariah knowing about it. Susan was distracted by the writhing toddler, whose reindeer antlers dangled off her head as she began chanting, "No, no, no."

She looked at me again with a hopeful expression. "Jim will be done soon," I said with a forced smile as I pulled Mariah out the door.

"We have a few minutes before our shift; I'm going to make a quick run to check a sale, then I'll meet you at Santa Land." I was already waving goodbye and walking away. She started to say something, then just waved back and veered over to a children's clothes store, where she liked to window-shop for foster sibling gifts.

I headed into a monolithic department store, on a mission. The best part of the elf costume was that it had a little bag on the belt, and I had thought ahead to put my debit card inside with my tiny phone.

My heart dropped a bit as I saw the grim line of people that snaked from the cashier. I would be late for work, but I wasn't changing course. They eyed me as I approached, either bored or suspicious of line jumpers.

Just past them, the purse department spread out in front of me like a cornfield maze. I was glad I knew where to find what I needed as I passed row after row of leather, vinyl, canvas, buckles, plain, pattern, fake snake . . .

The Bryce collection resided in a shrine-like alcove. The one I wanted, the one most like the camera bag, sat high on the right. Lit with little spotlights, it already looked too expensive.

I was cut off by a woman in the kind of chic suit women don't wear to work but to society events. She drifted over and picked up the bag. My bag. She frowned at it, flipping open the pockets and turning it over like it annoyed her.

So put it down. Down, down. Now. Was she going to buy it or not? She looked toward my feet, and I realized I was standing too close. If I rushed her decision, she might walk around the store with it while thinking it over.

I pushed myself forward, pretending to look at the other bags. Starting on a low shelf, I flipped over a price tag, my right hand twitching. My heart fluttered at the price, but I held my ground. I was getting her a good gift this time, one that would make up for all the cheap stuff I'd given her in the past.

I smiled at the woman, wanting to share my excitement, as silly as it might be. "They're gorgeous aren't they?" Chic suit woman ignored me. Maybe my costume made her think I was a store employee. Or a weirdo. I felt let down, but at least she put the bag back on its perch. I reached up for it. Mariah would be thrilled when she opened the box. My hand shook as I grasped the strap. Sheesh, how much caffeine did I have already?

Chic suit woman seemed to have no respect for personal space. A hand reached in front of me and jabbed at a bag. I leaned back, but the hand went with me. I stopped and stared. It was my hand, and it was moving on its own, twitching and jerking in front of me. Flashes of blue-white light blocked my vision, then cleared.

My legs collapsed under me, and I fell against the Bryce display, scattering handbags across the floor.

Chic suit woman recoiled, staring at me as if I had done something disgusting. As if I had a choice. My arm continued to jerk and scratch my nails across my face and other arm. The hairpins were pulling out hairs as my head rubbed against the floor. I had no control—it was as if my body had turned against me. The woman tried to step past me and slipped on a large shiny purse. She toppled to the floor.

She pulled herself up on her elbows, furious eyes meeting mine. And I saw it, inches from my face: an animal on the woman's throat. But not any kind of animal I had ever seen before. It was bright red-orange with a wide frog-like mouth frowning down at me. A ruff of plates like stiff feathers lifted around its neck as it breathed.

My head jerked to the side, obscuring my view. When I turned back, the woman was gone. But I could see through the display tables to the line at the cashier. The people couldn't see me easily from their angle. They must have thought the other woman had knocked the bags down and left. They mostly stared off into space.

And they all had little animals on them.

Ugly, creepy, frightening to look at. I closed my eyes. My jerking movements were subsiding, but I still couldn't move normally.

Panting, I opened my eyes again. The creatures were still there. I wasn't in any pain and there was nothing else I could do but look at the things. Surely they couldn't be real, but they looked so solid. Brilliant colors like macaws, and delicate shadings like the desert. Knobby skin and shiny. From the size of my thumb to as big as a human head. They varied in location too. One on a shoulder, another clinging to a belly, yet another—eww! The last man in line eyed the woman in front of him as she rocked back and forth, checking the line ahead of her. Seeing she was distracted, the man ogled her freely. And his little animal—well not that, but that's where the creature was clinging to him—seemed to tighten its grip, and the man's expression turned to a full-on leer as he ran his eyes down her butt.

I was still twitching, but fascinated. They were all menacing. Like evil frogs, or lizard men, or demons.

Demons? Of course; I'm hallucinating, why wouldn't it be something freaky?

Something wet touched my shoulder and face. I was drooling. Or foaming at the mouth. Could this possibly get any worse?

The cashier looked over her shoulder at the wrecked Bryce display. Her eyes followed it down to my twitching face, and she gasped. She called for security, the phone gripped against her shoulder, and pointed in my direction while a customer handed her a stack of fleece throws and a candle. Two people were doing something on their cell phones. Calling 911? *Please God, don't let anyone take a picture of me now.*

The cashier's voice came and went above the background hum of the mall. "I think she's having a seizure . . ."

Seizure? It had a name, what was happening to me. Maybe I wasn't dying. I was glad people weren't crowding around, but come on, one person could walk over to help.

"Well, hello there! Christmas shopping got you down? Sorry, but this is a no napping zone—store policy."

Ridiculous. No one would say that to someone in trouble. So now I'm hearing things too. But it wasn't a disembodied voice. A young man's face loomed above me, showing concern.

Oh, God. It was the tall cute guy, Shay. *And I'm dressed like an elf.*

He touched my face lightly. "Are you okay? Can you breathe all right?"

A second teen was on my other side, moving the fallen purses away from my jerking arms. I still had a death grip on the purse I had chosen. He pulled it gently away from me. I tried to stop him, to hold on to the purse, but couldn't. His eyes met mine, then went to Shay's as if for confirmation before he slid it out of my hand. His face was concerned and yet calm.

I couldn't speak, but Shay seemed satisfied I wasn't choking. A third teen appeared with public restroom-type brown paper towels. Like the other guy, this one treated Shay like a leader and handed the towels to him. Shay used them to wipe the spit off my face, then crumpled the towels away like it was routine. He looked around, appraising the bystanders, then down to my belt purse. "Is it okay if I check for a phone?" I looked down toward my belt, and he opened the purse. "I'm Shay, and that's Pierce and Garcia." He nodded toward each of them. "Let's see if we can call someone for you."

Pierce walked back and forth, putting away the bags. He stopped at Shay's shoulder and said, "She can't hear you."

Shay looked at me quizzically. "She can't? Why not?"

Pierce said, "She's having a seizure. People are unconscious during seizures. I learned that in a first aid class."

"Okay, let's see." Shay kept looking in my eyes. "Can you understand me?"

My mouth was as uncontrollable as my left arm, which was doing an impression of a dying fish. I tried to nod, but it was more like I was scratching my head with the floor. Finally, I blinked hard three times in a row.

Shay looked up at Pierce. "She understands me."

Well, that might be going too far, but I was nowhere near unconscious.

"That's what they told us in the class."

I realized these guys had no creatures on them. Why were they different? I looked back at the cash register line—none there either. I was so surprised I didn't notice that my body was finally lying still and I was moving my head voluntarily.

Then I heard the one ring and the electronic voice on the phone reading off the number and saying the owner was unavailable. Shay had called my ICE—"in case of emergency" contact—as one would in a situation like this.

"I think he blocked me," I said with a sigh. Well, he certainly hadn't wasted any time moving on. I got one phone call through to his voice mail last night after looking through the box. One call. Like when you go to jail.

Shay patted my arm. "You're feeling better now? A little? Don't get up." A light touch of his palm on my forehead pushed me back down. The now off-kilter elf hat pulled out a few more hairs. "The ambulance should be here any second. Who can I call to meet you at the hospital?"

"Mariah." My brain was working again. Working again? Was it not working right before?

He used the phone again. "Mariah, my name is Shay. Your friend . . . uh . . ." He looked to me.

"Eliana." It was too complicated. I reached for the phone. My hand was pulled back—Pierce was at my side again and patted my hand awkwardly while Shay spoke.

"Eliana had a seizure; we're waiting with her for an ambulance." He listened to frantic squawking from Mariah. "At Ridgepoint Mall, but I'll ask what hospital . . . oh, you're here? Uh, in Macy's, in the purse department, close to the um, pantyhose? Okay, see you in a minute."

Great, so much for the surprise gift. "Hey, where is the purse, the Bryce? It's for my best friend."

"No more shopping right now. Doctor's orders." Shay began tapping numbers again.

"I'm programming in my church's phone number, for emergencies. I would put in my number, but you might think I'm hitting on you." He winked at me. I sighed; I was dressed like a drooling elf and had no hope of Shay hitting on me.

Thundering footsteps preceded Mariah. I assured her I was okay, but Shay and Mariah refused to let me sit up.

The EMTs arrived, providing something new for the line of customers to gawk at. Shay squeezed my arm and said something encouraging, but I was distracted by a glimpse of myself in the mirrored side of a display case. My hair was teased up by my previous thrashing around, and the elf hat sat over one ear. With the smeared circles of elf blusher, I looked like a madwoman. Then Shay was gone.

The EMTs were thorough and didn't seem bothered that I appeared perfectly fine when they arrived. They asked what happened, and as much as I wanted to talk about it, to understand it, I couldn't bring up the hallucinations. Seeing Mariah's concerned face, plus the random strangers trying to act like they weren't watching, I just couldn't. Maybe in the ambulance.

But once inside, the siren was going and the EMTs were talking to each other in between checking on my condition. And what if they thought I was on drugs? I had never done drugs, but some people look for the simplest explanations. So I kept quiet.

At the emergency room, I handed over my insurance card to a bustling admitting clerk. Then there were tests with technicians coming and going. I decided to try and say something when I got to talk to one person, but that never seemed to happen either. The doctor, when I saw one, was flanked by a nurse and a medical student.

I decided the hallucinations were probably a one-time thing.

When I was finally allowed to go, Mariah charged up to me, irate that they had prevented her from going with me in the ambulance. My friend the tigress. She gave me a long hug, then kept her arm around my shoulders as we walked toward the automatic glass doors to the parking lot.

"I tried to call your mom, but I don't have her number. Do you want to call her now?"

My whole body tensed. "Absolutely not."

"She'll be more upset if you wait to tell her, won't she?"

"That's you, not her. If I tell her she'll come over tonight to pick me up. But she won't just coddle me, she'll nag me." I stopped in the lobby and faced her; she had to get this. "She can't know—I can't stay there. Mariah, please? Promise me." She looked sad but resigned. I started toward the door again. "I just want to go to bed. I want this day over with." Then I started to cry. Mariah all but tried to carry me out.

"Okay, okay. Shh, it'll be all right."

"How could I have two horrible days in a row?" My voice was slipping into a whine. "I was looking forward to being able to shop." It sounded so shallow, but was it too much to ask?

"You can shop tomorrow—well, maybe next week. The stores will still be full of crap in a week."

Mariah got me home with the assurance that my car would be fine at the mall overnight.

***

Later that evening, she looked down at me where I was curled in the corner of the sofa. "Feeling better?"

I smiled up at her. "I feel fine. Don't worry."

She settled into the comfy chair. "I could stay with you, just to be sure . . ."

Her bed was just on the other side of the living room wall from the sofa bed that had become "mine" after the Thanksgiving debacle. Surely that was close enough.

"You're not camping out in the living room, Mariah—you'll just hover over me all night, checking to see if I'm breathing."

"How about we leave the stove light on in the kitchen, just in case you fall out of bed or something and I have to check on you?"

I was too tired to argue. "Fine. But no hovering, okay?"

I was asleep right after my head hit the pillow. My last thought was an odd one: *Where are they now?*

5

Goblins

Morning light rocked across the foot of the bed as the tree branches outside the window swayed. My eyes fluttered and rested, half closed. Dreamy and peaceful. I thought of Shay at the store yesterday. Not the events, just his kind eyes. His quiet resolve to be helpful and treat me with dignity. I wondered why he would be so kind to a stranger. His lips, parting as he looked at me . . .

Suddenly, I was surrounded by small, goblin-like creatures. They grabbed at my legs, my arms, and scratched at my torso. My body was frozen, and a horrifying dread flowed through me. They pulled down, as if to pull me right through the mattress. *I'm dreaming; it's just a dream.* But at the same time, I could see the living room in the dim light, the deep pink duvet cover over my body, and my sweater draped over the far side of the sofa. Dreaming, or awake?

I struggled to sit up. If I sat up, I could make myself wake up. But my body refused to move. The goblins continued to pull downward. Where? To Hell?

Wake up, wake up, wake up. I was paralyzed.

Our Father who art in heaven . . . It was the only prayer I could think of, and my mind blanked after the opening. *Our Father, our Father . . .* My body jerked to one side, and all the little creatures ducked under pillows or into folds in the sheets and hid, just out of sight. I pushed myself into a sitting position. I was awake and alone in the room. My jeans and shirt and socks sat in a pile on the floor, looking strangely ordinary after the disturbing dream. Lifting a pillow revealed . . . nothing.

"That's enough weird stuff for this week," I said out loud. My muscles ached, and I felt bruised. The events of the previous day were coming back to me, eclipsing the best part—the strange, quirky man that seemed to have his own entourage. With a shudder, I pushed his memory from my mind, in case it brought back the goblins, though I didn't know why it would.

With a sigh, I wrestled my way out of the tangle of sheets and comforter, then headed to the bathroom while doing a mental inventory of the food in Mariah's fridge. I could cook breakfast for Mariah as a thank you.

It took a ton of conditioner to get the knots out of my hair in the shower. On my way to the kitchen, I peeked in at Mariah; she had left her door open so she could hear if I was in trouble. A one-bedroom apartment leaves little opportunity for sneaking around. Not much of Mariah was visible above her quilt except her eyes, and they were already open and appraising me. The quilt lowered to expose her mouth. "Feeling better?"

"Yes, well no—I felt fine yesterday." I leaned against the door-way as I thought. I was suddenly exasperated at the realization that there was no explanation for what happened. "I felt fine until my body went berserk for no apparent reason." I fought back tears of frustration.

Mariah shed the quilt and sprang up, crossing the room to me. I stared. There above Mariah's left breast was a little animal—creature—what the hell was it? It was like the ones I saw yesterday, not like the goblins of my dream. Mariah didn't notice the change in my expression and hugged me tightly. I didn't feel any object on her chest, but when Mariah pulled back, there it was. It didn't look up at me, just stared down at its own crablike claws, which were gripping Mariah's shirt. Or were they going through the material into her skin?

She put a hand on my face, gently lifting my chin.

"You're going to be fine. You are fine. If anything else happens, we'll get you back to a doctor. Okay?"

I tried not to stare at her chest. I couldn't just reach out and touch it without groping my friend. I stared down at the floor and nodded. With a final pat on my arm, Mariah dashed to the bathroom.

It couldn't be real, so why bother her with it? Maybe I was still getting over the seizure thing and it would stop soon. "Get you back to a doctor," she had said. I could go back to the emergency room without telling Mariah. It would give me some reassurance at least.

I groaned and headed off to the kitchen to root around in the fridge. It was full of reasonably healthy food for busy people. Boiled eggs, a carton of soy milk, and homemade vegetable pot pie were the highlights. Nothing sounded good.

Mariah appeared at my shoulder. Seeing the look on my face, she said, "Let's go out for breakfast."

With sudden inspiration, I said, "I've got Pop-Tarts," and stepped back from the fridge and swiped the back of my hand across Mariah's chest as I turned to the cabinet behind her. "Oh, sorry." I jerked my arm back again. I had felt nothing but the cotton of Mariah's T-shirt, yet the creature turned its ugly head to look up and scowl at me.

I forced myself to look away. "And I saw you have instant oatmeal in flavors." I jerked the cabinet door open and dug around for the box of oatmeal.

"Oatmeal, hmm, I'd rather not. Are you working today?"

"I was scheduled, but I texted Jim and he said to take some time off. I do want to go in and fill out a leave request so it's official that I'm not slacking." I met her eyes at last. Mariah looked tired.

"I have to drive you over there for your car anyway; we'll get something at the food court." Mariah was saving up her money, but she had friends at the mall who gave her free food. "If you're sure you're okay to drive?"

I assured her I was up to it. But even Mariah wouldn't have been able to keep me home for long. Sitting at home with my thoughts couldn't be good for me, nor could I risk losing a photog job.

I was already showered and dressed. Mariah detangled her hair, put on deodorant, and was ready to go. I found it amazing that a model could be so careless about her appearance.

***

As Mariah drove, it was easy to avoid looking at her. Even answering her questions could be done while looking intently out the windows.

At the mall, I insisted on checking on my car. No broken windows. I got my sunglasses from the front seat and wore them inside. The mall had just opened five minutes ago, but a throng of people milled about in the food court. Everywhere I looked, I saw little creatures—on backs, on heads, on their legs. Everyone seemed to have at least one, while some were crawling with them. I stopped looking.

While waiting for our to-go order from her friend, Mariah said, "Hey, you're wearing sunglasses inside." I muttered something about my eyes being sensitive to the light. Mariah looked concerned, but didn't pursue it.

We said goodbye outside the studio, and I hurried my bag of food past Susan at the front counter. When Jim had texted that I should take some time off, I said I would submit the sick leave form and then decide how long before I came back to work. I filled out the form and photocopied my doctor's note from the ER saying I should take time off. I put correction fluid on the part that said I shouldn't drive and copied it again. I got my camera from the locker and headed back out to the reception area, then killed some more time wiping my camera lenses to be sure Mariah had left the mall parking lot. She didn't need to know where I was going.

Susan had heard about my incident from Jim. I used my busyness to avoid her attempts at conversation. The woman wasn't good at picking up on social signals though, or she just ignored subtle signs and plowed on with giving me unwanted advice. I slipped out while her back was turned.

I was about to walk out the door to the parking lot when I did a U-turn and ran to the department store. I still didn't have the ruddy purse. I was breathless when I got to the purse department, but of course it was gone. I at least lucked out and found a free employee, but she swore up and down that everything they had was on the display. I headed again for the door.

Chic suit woman must have nabbed it while I was being carted off in the ambulance.

6

Doctor Revisit

The emergency room waiting area was empty, but this had given the staff an opportunity to take a meal break, so I still waited. I dug in my purse to get the name of yesterday's doctor.

The doctor showed no sign of being pleased to see me again. Gritting my teeth, I came out with it. "I'm hallucinating. I saw things yesterday during the seizure, and I'm seeing them again today."

"Flashes of light, spots, that sort of thing?"

"No, actual things . . . like . . ." *Like that scaly thing with its tail wrapped around your neck.*

"Did you hit your head?

". . . lizards. You asked that yesterday." It was out before I realized I was saying it. I needed to get information from her, not act like I knew it all.

The doctor's lips grew thinner. She flicked her penlight in and out of my eyes with unnecessary curtness. She stepped back and rattled off a list of reasons for hallucinations, some potentially harmless, some not. She told me I'd just have to watch it, and that it would be best to go to a neurologist for further tests, or talk to my regular doctor otherwise.

"I don't have a regular doctor." Again, it slipped out. The doctor didn't seem to think that was her problem, but I had to get my questions answered before she hurried off. The smoky black creature on her neck seemed to frown at me.

"And while it was happening yesterday, someone said it wasn't a seizure because I was still conscious. Is that right?"

"There are different types of seizures, with different levels of consciousness. Who said that?"

"A guy who was helping me."

She met my gaze. I guessed that look meant she didn't think "the guy" was qualified.

"Hmm." She scribbled a note in my folder. Was she writing "hmm" or some doctor equivalent? *Is there a word for "hmm" in Latin?*

She whipped out her prescription pad, wrote and ripped off three prescriptions, then handed them to me as she stepped toward the door. Said something about following up if things didn't return to normal, and that if it didn't clear up, it could be psychological and therapy would be in order. She opened the door and was gone.

"Hmm." I looked at my purse and coat, crumpled on the chair. Nothing crawling around on them. I looked down at myself. Nothing on me either. If I was hallucinating, why was it so inconsistent?

***

I sat in my car and looked at the prescriptions. The scrawl was hard to read, but they seemed to be for headaches, sleeplessness, and anxiety. Did I say I had any of those? Maybe anxiety, but doesn't everyone? An image of Shay singing Christmas carols as he strolled through the mall popped up in my memory. Okay, normal people have anxiety.

I dropped the prescriptions on the passenger seat and blew the hair out of my eyes. Mariah might be studying at the apartment, and I didn't want to lie on the couch with my thoughts anyway. I started driving.

My mom would look after me if I went home, but she would also smother me. It would start as care, then there would be little snide barbs of criticism mixed in, and if I tried to stand up for myself, it would become a fight. It took a year of reading self-help books to figure out that she was acting out all her problems on me, and there was nothing I could do to fix the situation. I just had to find ways to deal with her, and right now having some distance seemed the easiest way.

I wasn't always so angry and bitter. I had been a good student in school, and I had a small group of close friends. I guess what bugged me about Mom was that she kept trying to control me instead of letting me make my own choices. And what bugged me about Chas was that he somehow got around my mental radar. I thought I was good at reading people, so how had I been so wrong about him?

Taking pictures always made me feel better, so I pulled off the road to a tiny taco stand with outdoor seating. I got my camera from the trunk and started exploring. I started with some clear shots of the location, but anything was fair game once I got rolling. I liked taking closeups of the ordinary and the ugly. Decaying windows or grackles eyeing me suspiciously or a flower growing through cracked pavement were my favorite kinds of subjects. One small item becomes the star when you zoom in on it. It's human nature to look for a story in what we see, so the photographer doesn't have to create a story, just give the basis for the viewer to start creating.

My own story had some glaringly blank pages now. After the disaster that was Thanksgiving Day, Mom was adamant that she wouldn't help pay for art school, but I didn't have a Plan B. The studio job would drop to part-time hours in January, and wouldn't be enough to support me entirely. The change of plans had left me feeling off-balance.

The taco stand proprietor was leaning against the door and watching me. It wasn't lunchtime, so I wasn't taking a customer's parking spot, but I bought a Coke from her. Keeping my eyes on the counter allowed me to avoid looking at the crimson reptilian thing clinging to her chest. The two cooks sat and smoked under a tree at the side of the building. People are more interesting subjects, but I was often shy about photographing strangers if they weren't performers. The primitive people were right; it felt like stealing a piece of their soul. It's probably why celebrities get so messed up. It has to be a trade, some of yourself for some of what they have. And I was protective of my own little bits of soul.

I squatted down at the edge of the cracked parking lot and took a closer look. A bare section of dirt was crisscrossed with bird footprints. I wasn't sure how well they would show up, but I took a few pictures.

It was getting chilly, but I was having fun taking pictures of a dog that had wandered by, then of smiley faces I drew on my styrofoam cup. And not once did I hallucinate with the inanimate objects or the dog—only with the people.

7

Telling Mariah

The next morning, I lay in bed, reluctant to move. But I had to go really bad. I opened my eyes and gave my body and the room a quick once-over. No goblins. I jumped up and headed for the bathroom, nearly running into Mariah as she came out. We both jumped a little, which is good because she didn't notice I was startled to see . . . nothing. No weird creature clutching at her this morning. We mumbled good mornings and she headed back to bed.

"Hey," I said, "shopping today!"

She grumbled in response, "No shopping, decorating."

The store closest to me didn't have her bag anyway, so shopping might as well wait. "Okay, decorating, but no singing."

***

Later that morning I tapped away at Mariah's computer, doing freelance work, uploading files to a stock photo website and adding tags to them while she sang off-key Christmas carols.

Mariah's was a complicated story I could never keep straight. She loved being a big sister, but with her foster parents having a lot of younger kids to look after, money was short. She had a college scholarship, but still had to pay for all her living expenses and keep her grades up between part-time jobs. She would start law school next year, and it was a pretty sure thing that this time she would receive the full-ride scholarship she deserved. However, it would probably be out of state. I got a tight feeling in my stomach at the thought of losing her.

"Hey, you said you wanted a normal, happy, family-type Christmas, so get over here and decorate."

I clicked save and looked at what she was doing. She was hanging big swooping garlands of fake pine along one wall of the living room. A pile of posterboard and art supplies lay in the middle of the floor.

"There's no tree." I really had no idea what she was planning to do with all that stuff.

"Not yet." She pushed the garland higher with a grunt and placed it on a plastic hook. "We'll get the tree from my folks by next week. Decide what you want to decorate it with; I only have a few ornaments."

I wandered over. She was way taller, so I couldn't help with the garland.

"What's all this posterboard?"

"A fireplace." She glanced over her shoulder. "It'll be cute. Really."

The drapey garland was pre-decorated with red Christmas ornament balls and red poinsettias. I rubbed my eyes; the red areas seemed to be blurring and moving. I had a small, panicky feeling in the back of my head.

Mariah announced, "It's done," and stomped down the ladder. She turned toward me with a smile, and I yelped. The orange *thing* was there again, clutching at her chest. I had the urge to draw back and to rush forward to knock it off at the same time, causing me to lurch drunkenly where I stood.

That only made Mariah rush toward me, her . . . creature along for the ride. She grabbed my arms as if I might fall. I just stared, aghast, at the creature clawing at her.

"Eliana!" she yelled, shaking me till I met her eyes. "What's wrong?"

A lie came to my mind first. *Just say I'm nauseated, or the doctor said it's normal to have dizziness.* But without looking at her, I told the truth. "I may have something really bad wrong with me."

She pushed me toward the couch, then grabbed her phone. "I'm calling an ambulance."

"No! Please, no. Let me explain." I had to look at the floor to think straight. "Just sit here, I'll tell you."

She sat next to me on the couch and waited, breathless.

"I don't want you to worry." She started to wave that away, but I said, "Not for you, for me. I don't want you hovering around me or you will drive me nuts." We both laughed, me with tears running down my face. She gave me a quick hug and waited again.

"I see . . . things on people. Hallucinations . . . I guess. They are like weird lizard creatures, but evil looking. Like demons."

She kept her voice calm. "Everywhere you look?"

"No." I still didn't understand this part myself. "Just on people." I could tell from her expression she didn't get it. "On their shoulders, speaking into their ears, or on their hands if they are doing something. Sometimes holding a part of their body. And they see me too. They look me right in the eyes."

Mariah was acting calm, but her eyes were wide. "Uh huh."

"See, I didn't want you to think I'm crazy."

She gave me a firm hug.

"Maybe I am. Crazy."

She didn't stop hugging me, but she took a long time to answer.

"It's okay, Ellie." She saved that nickname for when I was at rock bottom, like when Chas dropped the breakup bomb on me. "There are people who can help you."

"Like . . . ?"

She pulled back from the hug now, wiping her eyes and sniffling. "I can call my family and ask who they used. You know, when the fosters needed someone."

My stomach dropped. I had assumed she would simply laugh off the "crazy" suggestion and we would go on from there.

"You think I need a psychiatrist?"

"A counselor." She saw my expression and talked faster. "We all need some guidance sometimes. They just help you get through a bad time. Like with you and Chas and your mom . . . the new job. It's probably all that stress, El."

I didn't know how to tell her that I felt not-crazy even though I was seeing something that sounded like crazy was the only explanation. Was that how people felt when they have severe mental issues? Did they feel normal? I had always thought that at least one little corner of your brain would be in on what was really happening.

"Okay, even if it's just to rule that out. I'll go."

She looked down and her face changed. Looking back up, face tense, she said, "What about on me? Did you see . . . anything on me?"

"The first morning after it happened." I knew she would keep asking so I went on, "And now. Just one. Right here." I pointed to a spot above my left breast, not wanting to look at her creature to point to it. "It's orange and bumpy and has little claws clutching at you."

I noticed she didn't put her hand on the spot, or even look there.

"Tell me if you see another one."

I promised.

Ten minutes later—the time it took us to make hot chocolate and spread scissors, colored markers, and poster paints all over the living room—we were bent over the posterboard. I cut strips of construction paper to make chains while Mariah painted the background for our red brick fireplace.

"Are you sure this is how grown-ups celebrate Christmas in their swinging bachelorette pads?"

"Yes, yes. Keep going." She chose a new paintbrush to add details to the mock brickwork.

We built our fake fireplace out of paper and paint and stuck it to the wall to pretend we had a house Santa could visit. Despite my promise, I vowed not to discuss demons with her again. She was one of the few happy parts of my life, and I didn't want to ruin that by scaring her.

8

Dr. Linda

Monday morning, everything was normal. No weird dreams and no creatures on my roommate. I didn't trust it though. It was like walking on eggshells, and my shoulders were sore from the tension of waiting for something to appear.

I arrived at the mall, still wearing my sunglasses inside and avoiding looking at people. The doctor had suggested taking a week off work, but I didn't want to sit home all day. The original plan had been to work as many hours as possible to save up a little more money and then to drop to part time in January when I started school. Jim scheduled me for extra studio work instead of the elf job so I wouldn't have to be in a crowded area. He was being thoughtful, and I wanted to show him that I was a good employee. Or maybe he was worried the kids would see an elf collapse. Despite my initial dread at the idea of working as an elf, I felt bad about not doing it.

I walked through the Santa court with my coffee shop treat, which was much better today—I even got all the frou-frou stuff on top. But that made it harder to sip casually while staring into the distance, so I ended up making eye contact with the Santa photographer. I was worried the other staff would be annoyed that I wasn't doing my share of work there. He had his arm draped around an elf and smiled at me and waved as he said something in her ear. She smiled and waved too, so I told myself to stop being paranoid. I continued walking and sipping casually and got whipped cream on my face.

***

Days went by, all was still well, and I told Jim I was ready for Santa Land. Even then I didn't get to see Mariah as much as I had hoped—she studied more than she worked. But when we did get to be elves on the same shift, it was fun.

I called Mom to apologize for Thanksgiving and for not returning her calls. I also let her know there were a couple emergency room bills coming in that I would pay and she should not worry about. Just an abundance of caution after I fell in a department store.

By the beginning of the next week, I was starting to forget the whole thing. Hours would go by without my wondering what I would see when I looked up at someone. I was starting to think about what I would do in January. I didn't have to be tied to my old plans with Chas now that he was gone. I was free to do whatever I wanted. But I wanted to know what he was up to. What could that hurt, right? Was he working? Was he dating someone else? Was that the real reason he left? While Mariah was taking a nap, I used her computer to social media stalk Chas, his friends, his mom, and any and all acting schools in Chicago, but couldn't find anything useful. What a creep; he wouldn't even give me the satisfaction of finding out about him secretly.

***

After getting my hopes up for being normal again, I woke up with a bad feeling in my belly. Not a stomachache, but more a foreboding.

When I heard Mariah coming out of the bathroom, I dragged myself out of bed. "Good morn . . ." Yes, there was her little hitchhiker, back in place. Fortunately, I was able to act sleepy, and she didn't notice how upset I was. Her dad had made an appointment for me to see a therapist that afternoon, and I had decided to go whether I seemed normal or not. Good thing I didn't cancel.

Dr. Linda Boudreaux's office was not in the best part of town, meaning I could better handle whatever the insurance didn't pay. There was no parking lot on the busy street, so I had to park some distance away and walk past the sleepy storefronts turning golden in the fading light. A bus roared by, the inside lit as if it were a house interior on a cozy evening.

Her practice was on the ground floor of a quaint Victorian. The polished wood floors squeaked and the doors needed a hard push to close, but it had high ceilings that made me feel more relaxed somehow. Not closed in.

Dr. Boudreaux brought me into her inner office with very little fuss about paperwork and settled me into a firm leather chair. I gave her the condensed version of my "episode."

"What is the story on the 'in case of emergency' ex-boyfriend?"

I didn't even take a breath; I might have held it and never spoken. I just let it all gush out, barely even hearing my own words. It was like listening to myself on the radio.

I told her that I met him in the same acting class where I met Mariah. That he'd visited his aunt in Chicago months ago, but never mentioned thinking of moving. How I didn't want to leave Houston, but would have considered it . . . but it turned out he didn't want me to go with him.

I told her how Mariah's friendship got me through the shock of it. Most of my friends had been his friends first, so I no longer saw them. Not that I would mind seeing most of them, but I dreaded the idea that they might pity me. How I worried that he went to Chicago because he had already found someone else. The worst was that tiny part that hoped he was miserable, because that meant it mattered to me, and I didn't want it to matter. How things always ended up like this, with me like an abandoned dog on the side of the road, wondering when the car is coming back.

Every time I finished speaking, she continued to stare at me, almost unblinking. It was disconcerting. I felt pressured to say more.

"But that's not why I'm here."

"Maybe it is," she said. "You desperately want attention from the boyfriend who left you. So your mind creates the attention-getting state; even the so-called hallucinations give attention to you."

Dr. Linda said what I was seeing were not true hallucinations, but manifestations of feelings of guilt and fear that I wouldn't admit to myself. She went through a long explanation of how and why, and different ways those feelings could manifest—dreams, physical ailments like pain, fainting, whatever . . . then she said, pen poised over my file, "Or maybe you hit your head?"

Maybe I can hit you on the head and plead insanity. Shaking my head, I tried to look interested.

Dr. Linda gave me a handful of mantras to say to remind myself of what was real and what wasn't, like: "There is no demon there, because demons don't exist."

"But," I asked, "don't they? I mean, I shouldn't see them, but aren't there . . . ?"

Dr. Linda turned on her warmth and touched my forearm. "Do you believe they are there?"

"Well, no." I grappled with my thoughts to put them into words. "Not what I'm seeing, but aren't demons really out there, or in Hell?" I waited while she stared back unblinkingly at me through her dark-rimmed glasses.

"The only thing out there is you—what you believe—in some form that your mind is using to try to understand the world. Do you see that?"

I saw. I saw a demon peering up at the doctor. It was gripping her arm just above her wrist, and it had one lizard-like leg stretched forward on her hand. "Does this time work for you, with your work schedule? We could meet this same time each week. Eliana!"

I jumped back, startled at the sharp tone. Dr. Linda had noticed that I was staring at her arm.

"There is no demon there," Dr. Linda began, "because demons— let me hear you say it."

"Don't exist?" I said meekly, concentrating on her face.

"Good. The whole thing now."

I had to chant the whole thing plus a couple more for practice, such as "I'm hallucinating, and it will stop soon. I am getting well." I could still see the one on her arm, but she said therapy takes time.

I managed to leave without agreeing to more sessions. Either I hit my head and it would go away on its own, or—whatever. I didn't want this woman in my head with or without the demons in there. I believed demons existed, but had never believed they pop up in "real life." One summer when one of my friends had a religious awakening I read the whole Bible, front to back. But I couldn't keep up the same enthusiasm she had. I believed God was real and he loved me, but he was far away. It was like all religious stuff belonged in a separate part of my life that I never got around to dealing with. Now something was creeping through the crack under the door.

Outside the office, everything looked different. What had been a busy city street at sunset was now deserted. The sleepy store-fronts seemed forbidding. And confusing. I was so preoccupied while walking to the office I hadn't paid attention to how far away I parked or what the cross street was.

Just ahead, a skinny man with a graying beard sat on a brick planter. His plaid coat was not enough for the cold breeze. He stared vaguely at the ground and was holding a bottle in a brown paper bag. A mournful, bloated demon with pouchy eyes sat on his shoulder like a reptilian possum. I noted that the demon must be an alcohol dependency demon, then scolded myself—there is no such thing. *I'm hallucinating, and it will stop soon. I will get well.*

I stuffed my hands further into my pockets and strode forward, looking straight ahead like I knew where I was going. Nearby, I saw a man getting out of an SUV, brushing his wool coat and adjusting his scarf. He looked like an L.L. Bean model, except that he had demons clinging to him, front and back.

No he doesn't. He can't, because they don't exist.

"Excuse me," I said to him. My hands were getting stiff with cold now. The man glanced down the block before meeting my eyes. His largest demon was holding his throat and speaking into his ear. Well, no it wasn't, because they don't exist.

"I know I parked on Whitby, but I'm turned around. Do you know which way it is?" I followed his roaming gaze to see if the skinny man was coming up behind me, but there was no one in sight. I turned back to find the catalog model looming over me, close enough that the smell of the wool coat assaulted my nostrils.

His face was blank, like he hadn't understood. "I parked on Whitby," I said again, a bit exasperated and taking a small step back.

Everything I had been taught about self-defense failed me. The man's grip was like concrete on my arm; I had no hope of twisting away from it. I couldn't jab his solar plexus through his winter coat or reach his Adam's apple while being propelled forward to an SUV that had been backed diagonally into a parking space.

I was so surprised that I only gasped at first, and had to make myself scream, "Help me!" The sound echoed off the empty buildings.

He pulled faster, eagerness breaking through the blank façade of his face.

What else? What else can I do? My mind was starting to panic, and telling myself not to panic was creating a feedback loop of numbing helplessness.

He beeped the door lock open. Reached for the door handle. So well-choreographed. But maybe if I made it hard enough, he would give up. I dropped to my knees and screamed, "Help me!" again. Maybe someone was there after all.

He flung the door open and turned to haul me up like baggage. A flash of light glittered in front of me like the reflection off a pool of water, and the man fumbled as he grabbed for my other arm. He seemed surprised at the hiccup, and the demon on his neck looked frenzied. The light came again, and this time I thought I saw—

Please, not more hallucinations.

It was almost like, in that brief flash, a translucent winged man, taller than my attacker, had jumped in and grabbed the demon's face, making it loosen its hold on the man's throat. Without thinking, I stood and swiped my nails at the man. He dodged, and since he still held my coat with one hand, knocked me back to my knees. He pulled back his fist, and my stomach turned over, knowing I was going to have my first ever punch in the face and it was going to be terrible.

The sound of glass breaking caused him to look up. I was afraid to take my eyes off him, but I turned enough to look beside me. The skinny man stood there with a broken bottle in his hand.

"You get out of this place! You get away from her—you hear me?" He thrust the bottle forward, and my attacker pulled back. He and his demon sneered in unison, but he let go. I fell backward and scuttled away like a crab.

"Go, get out now, and don't you come back here!"

The attacker gave him a look of disdain, but he slid into the open door and started the SUV. The man helped me stand, then pulled me well out of the way as the SUV roared off into the night.

The man, he said his name was Major, pulled his hand away as soon as I was steady on my feet. He made bits of small talk, examining my face as he walked me to Whitby Street and my car. Tears ran down my cheeks as I walked numbly along, not bothering to wipe them away. I couldn't think of words sufficient to thank him, but he waved my attempts away and stood guard until my car pulled out into the street.

His demon—that wasn't supposed to exist—was half the size it had been earlier.

9

Church

I parked in a busy drugstore parking lot, by a large intersection. I always lock my doors, but I checked them two or three times as I sat in the car. Every time a man looked my direction a little too long, I felt jumpy. I called 911, and they asked if I wanted an officer to come out. I didn't think there was much point taking them to the site, so I told them all I could on the phone. Without the license plate number, what I had wasn't much.

I didn't want to go home alone yet, but I had nowhere else to be. Mariah was out this evening. Plus, despite my promise to give her any updates on my problem, I didn't want to burden her. She was my only good friend these days. I had spent so much time working toward a future with the ex that I hadn't noticed my transition from "independent" to "isolated."

Near the drugstore entrance, two teenage boys scrolled through the Redbox selections, arguing over movie choices. I couldn't see any demons on them. So the . . . whatever this was; vision, or sight? Yes, the sight had turned itself off again. *Could it be turning on when*

I need it? The teen with ruffled brown hair laughed loudly. He made me think of Shay. Shay had given me his church's phone number.

My family had gone to church every Sunday . . . until Dad left. Mom kept taking us for a while, then said she was too busy, but she probably just didn't want to keep answering questions about Dad. Soon, we moved to a new neighborhood and the old church was too far away.

I missed the fun stuff at Sunday school most. It was like being at school with your friends, but with no homework. And they gave us cookies and juice every week.

Mom still believed in a kind of religious perfectionism, only talking about God when some kind of bad behavior was in question, but without the Sunday school coloring books and juice and cookies. And Dad either didn't find what he needed at church, or he was still out looking for Jesus. But I was running out of options.

I picked up my phone and scrolled through the contacts until I came to *"Hey Call This Number Eliana."* I grinned in spite of myself and hit dial. A dignified male voice answered with the name of the church; that couldn't be Shay.

I wanted to blurt out everything, but then, I still wasn't sure what had happened. I told him the bare minimum. "I had some kind of spasm or seizure, then started seeing demons on everyone. But not all the time, just sometimes, and I just almost got raped or killed and there was a flash of light that looked like an angel, then I was saved by a guy whose demon got smaller after he helped me." I sucked in a huge breath. "That's what you do, right? Deal in angels and demons?"

I could feel the weighty pause before he spoke, and knew he was choosing his words carefully. He suggested I come to the church, explaining they had a weekly group session that might help. Tears rolled down my face again as the helplessness rolled over me.

"I tried therapy. I didn't like the therapist much." Inspiration struck. "What about an exorcism?" I could already hear a "no" in the way he cleared his throat, but I pursued it. "I mean, it's usually a psychological thing anyway, right? The exorcism would just help my brain get the message there's nothing there! Simple."

One more small throat clearing. "Not being an expert in that arena, it's hard for me to say, but I think going into it as a psychological exercise would negate any possible benefit from an . . . exorcism. I believe the group dynamic would help; why not just visit and see?"

I jotted the info on a scrap of paper and agreed to give it a try. "Oh, one more thing," I said as an afterthought, "do you have a youth group?"

"We do," he said, "but I'm sorry, they don't meet tonight."

"That's fine." I was relieved that I wouldn't run into Shay again, cute though he was. Or because he was cute.

But when I hung up, I sat still. As the shakiness of the adrenaline waned, feelings of anger and disgust were emerging. Annoyance that I even had to go to these people for help. Dr. Linda, the church, any of them. They were no better than me at telling me how to live or how to think. What good does it do to be nice? Might as well be the one doing the hurting—they get away with it.

I shook myself. Where did that come from? After effects of the attack, maybe? I could ask at the church. *More therapy, bleah.*

***

The River of Hope parking lot was well lit, and there were plenty of people in the hallways of the education building. Children raced down the hall. Adults hung out in twos and threes. I looked at my note: Room 103. Even though the sight was off, I avoided making eye contact with anyone; I wasn't in the mood for small talk.

A short hall branched off to my left. I saw a water fountain and went for a long drink. A clapping or marching noise sounded from the last classroom. I edged past the fountain to peek around the door.

A guy with a gray hoodie pulled over his head had his back to me and was clapping while two teenage boys did pushups. At a bark from him, they jumped up and shadow boxed, then jogged in place. One of the teens looked familiar.

The guy in the hoodie called out, "What do we do?"

Still jogging, the teens responded as one, "We serve the Lord!"

Hoodie guy yelled back, "When do we do it?"

"All the time!"

I pulled back and slipped away to the main hall, their voices echoing after me.

"What do we do?"

"We serve the Lord!"

I saw a sign on Room 103 that read *"Dialogues on Healing."* But I couldn't go in. It was like my body was frozen again. I couldn't open myself up again so soon, this time to a whole group of strangers, and probably get no help. To stay out of the hallway traffic, I moved to lean against the wall by the door. Frustration tightened my chest and constricted my breathing. How was I ever going to fix this thing and get on with my life?

A sign across the hall caught my attention: *"Room 102—Spiritual Gifts Meeting."* A spiritual gift? Could that be what I had? All the events of the evening rearranged themselves in an instant. Not one unfortunate event after another, but the very problem I was trying to solve actually warning me of danger. Even arriving here, at this meeting, maybe this was part of it. Of course, I wouldn't have been in danger if I hadn't gone to the therapist to try to get rid of the problem. Still, it was an intriguing idea. And there are others with "gifts"? I was amazed at the possibility.

I walked into the classroom. Ten sets of eyes turned to me. A chunky, middle-aged man was passing out papers.

"Hi, can I sit in on this group? I . . . I think I may have a . . . a gift." Their warm smiles welcomed me, and one man jumped up to bring another chair into the circle.

The leader said, "You can't just 'sit in,' but you can be part of our group. I'm Bill, and we'll do introductions again at the break, Miss . . . ?"

"Eliana."

He handed me a set of stapled papers. "Okay Eliana, this is a guideline for the group, and a list of gifts the others have filled in. If you decide it's not for you, then I'll need this back, because it's kind of personal."

"Sure, of course, it's not something just anyone would understand." My heart leaped when I saw that some of the members had rather long lists of gifts by their names. I scanned the lists—did they have healing or demon exorcism? Maybe someone else saw spiritual beings? I was crushed to see that their spiritual gifts turned out to be things like *good with the grandchildren* or *patient with teaching people.* This can't be it. I flipped the page. *"Knit baby blankets for charity." "Good listener."* The others were skimming over the list as well and seemed content with it.

Bill had settled into his chair. "Now, Joe," he said gently, "I noticed you wrote 'like to read' on your list. I just think that is more of a hobby than a spiritual gift."

Joe, a crusty looking old guy, twisted his mouth further and said gruffly, "Well, Caroline put that she's good with her grandchildren, how is that not a hobby?" A frail old woman next to me folded her arms and looked away.

Bill said, "Anytime we relate to other people, we have a chance to share the . . . but okay, we'll come back to that later."

A smile on her wizened face, Caroline turned to me and put a hand on my arm. She asked, "And what's your gift, sweetie?"

Looking for a way out, I said, "It's reading," and headed for the door, leaving the list of gifts in my chair.

Bill called after me, "That's okay, we can discuss it." Someone, I suspect Joe, coughed pointedly.

Frustrated and with nowhere to go, I turned down the hall toward the water fountain again in case Bill came looking for me. I pretended to read the bulletin board to hide my tears and figure out what to do next.

Two of the young guys who had been doing pushups earlier walked out of their room and stopped as they saw me wiping tears off my face. I heard one whisper, "Should we do something?"

The other one grabbed the whisperer and hauled him into the men's room. I could still hear their fervent, quiet conversation. "We should pray for her." A thump on the tiles suggested he had dropped to his knees. A more muffled thump suggested the first one had kicked him.

"We should pray *with* her."

Great, I was being rescued by the Abbott and Costello apostles.

More scuffling noises. "What if we ask her and she says no? It could be something personal."

"Of course it's something personal, why would she cry about something that's not personal?" The bathroom door creaked as it opened a crack.

I had nothing further to keep me there, but I was curious about anyone so terrified of me. I continued reading the notices—children's Christmas pageant rehearsal, book club schedule, Christmas services—

"Pierce! Garcia! Break's over." It was the same voice that had been barking orders during the workout. The names seemed familiar. I turned to see—oh, not him.

Down the hall, a tall guy leaned out of the door. His gray hoodie was pushed back off his messy brown hair. The guy who had seen me with my body spazzing, my hair wild, and then wiped drool off my face. The last person I wanted to ever see again, my most humiliating and frightening moment permanently entwined with his enticing eyes: Shay.

I turned to escape down the hall, but the word *"demons"* scrawled in marker across a yellow flyer caught my attention. I hesitated. It featured an angel with a broken wing and the name Jon Addison. I reached to pull it down and take it with me, then jumped back as a hand smacked the page and yanked it off the board. I spun and found myself face-to-face with Shay. I felt weak. He had a little unshaven scruff on his chin, and his tousled hair unjustly made him even cuter. I considered walking away without saying anything.

"This guy is dangerous." He tossed the flyer into a trash can. I looked longingly after it. "Focusing on demons won't bring good into your life. You have to focus on good to get good things."

"But what if demons are what you see?" I blurted out, and was relieved to see he wasn't shocked by it.

"Then you need to look deeper. I can show you how to do that. Why don't you join us?"

He beckoned as he turned and strode down the hall. I wavered. The two sheepish guys came out of the bathroom and skulked down the hall. Had they prayed for me in there? I wasn't sure how I felt about that. I turned to walk away.

Shay called after me, "I have your purse."

I held my purse up high and kept walking.

"The Bryce one you wanted to buy at the mall. With the mountains and clouds."

I wasn't even aware of doing it, but I turned and stared at him. "How—how would you know . . ."

"Look deeper."

"You lost me."

That mischievous smile turned up his lips. "Then I shall find you again. Follow me." He crooked his finger at me and disappeared into the doorway. I followed.

10

The Youth Room

I stood on the threshold looking in.

The room turned out to be a combination of classroom and teen lounge. Storage too, judging by the stack of cardboard boxes in the corner. The classroom chairs were moved back, leaving floor space for the workout I glimpsed earlier. Old, comfy, upholstered chairs and a sofa were grouped around a coffee table on the far side of the room. A pink flamingo lamp perched on a side table, towering over two tissue boxes. Shay sat on the coffee table. The other two stood near him, more like soldiers than teens hanging out.

"Shay Davis." He waved toward each of the others as he introduced them, "You've met Pierce and Garcia—we use their last names because they're both named Justin. Dylan Parker, the fourth member of our team, is working tonight."

"Eliana Williams."

I wanted to trust Shay. Mostly. Sorta.

I walked closer to them. "What is this place? I know it's a church, but . . . what are you doing here?"

"This"—Shay swept his arms out to take in the whole room—"is our little corner of the church."

Garcia added, "We are a dedicated and detonated team of Jesus freaks, setting the world afire with the Holy Spirit." He high-fived Pierce, and they jumped onto the sofa in unison.

Shay frowned. "Guys, don't scare the newbie."

I moved around behind the chairs, looking at the graffiti on the side tables. No bad words, of course. One part of the coffee table was piled with plastic boxes of beads, cord, and fasteners. I leaned over for a closer look. Someone had been making What Would Jesus Do? bracelets. A small wicker basket held a handful of finished bracelets, like the one I had when I was a kid.

"Jesus freaks," Pierce echoed.

I glanced over the assortment of books on the bookcase and took a step back toward the door. "Yeah, freaks. Okay, good to know."

"We do volunteer work," Pierce spoke up, sounding a little hurt. "We feed the homeless, and do anti-bullying programs, and we talk to people, people who need . . ." Shay looked at him encouragingly. "People who need someone to talk to," he finished, looking at his hands.

"I started an offshoot of the youth program here at River of Hope for kids who want more opportunities to volunteer and do mission work."

"And you're their drill sergeant?"

He smiled. "If they had gotten here on time, they could have worked out with me. We train like we're being sent on a mission, because we believe that we are. Everyone has a mission. I want to be ready when I'm called, and I've taken it upon myself to give others opportunities to prepare for theirs. In a safe place."

"What's your current mission?"

Pierce spoke up again, "Tonight we're helping to clean up after the meetings because the janitor is sick. We're open to more exciting opportunities, but we're sixteen, and Shay's eighteen. They won't let us have a helicopter till we're older."

Garcia mumbled something about the unfairness of it.

Shay laughed and shook his head. He looked at ease, here in his domain, but I had a feeling he never felt out of place.

"What brought you here tonight, Eliana?" He patted the sofa cushion in front of him. Pierce and Garcia hopped off their sofa to the floor and started stringing beads onto bracelet cords. I relented and sat down, dropping my purse and coat next to me. *If I tell them and they think I'm crazy, I can just walk out.* Earlier I was going to walk out and never see them again anyway.

I felt a daring born of exhaustion—didn't I almost die an hour ago? I got to the point. "How do you kill a demon?"

Shay laughed. "You don't. They aren't physical beings, so they have nothing to be except what they are."

"Okay, then I need to get rid of them. Exorcism. How do I do one of those?"

Shay glanced back at the Justins. A swift, silent communication went on between them. He turned back to me and cleared his throat.

"I'm no expert in that. Supposedly," he said, then cleared his throat again, "you ask the demon its name and tell it to come out in the name of Jesus."

"That's it? Do that now, for me."

"Eliana, you're not possessed." His voice sounded funny. "Let's just take a step back. Tell me what's going on."

They had seen the seizure, but I caught them up on the high points of the drama in my life: the breakup, leaving home, the failed photography school plan, seeing demons off and on. All the way to that evening's attack. Garcia looked at Shay several times when I talked about the demons. Shay's face was unreadable as he looked at my fading bruises and scratches from the incident at the mall. New red marks on my arms from earlier in the evening mingled with them. They didn't ask questions while I talked.

At the end, I sighed. "I didn't hit my head, I don't do drugs, I'm not suffering from guilt . . . I even thought for a moment that maybe it was some kind of special power, so I tried the spiritual gifts group down the hall. This doesn't seem to be anything but a nuisance." I shrugged, not really sure what anyone could do for me.

"I can teach you some things that might help you. I can't promise that you'll stop seeing demons, though—that would depend on why you're seeing them in the first place," Shay said.

He had no idea, any more than the doctor or therapist. I felt tears of frustration welling up again. I tried to wipe them away by pretending to scratch my face. Garcia grabbed a tissue box to hand to Shay, then went back to work on his bracelet. Shay set the box on my lap. I dabbed my eyes with a tissue as Shay's voice lulled me into a relaxed state.

"Be aware of your body, your feelings, your surroundings. See what is there."

"So I know the difference between what's real and what isn't, right?"

"Demons are real. I'm trying to teach you how to not be hurt by them."

I held a tissue to my drippy nose, still trying to process what he just said. "The demons I see are real? As simple as that?"

"Are those particular ones real? We'll figure that out eventually," Shay said. "First, concentrate on the one thing you are most upset about. Close your eyes and see yourself letting it go."

"Let go? But if I could have done that . . ."

"Let go, let God." Garcia chimed in. My face must have shown my bewilderment.

Shay nodded. "Let go of everything; let God handle it. It's terrifying to most, the idea of giving up control, to let God work through you. In our world it's seen as death, the loss of self. But it's just your ego you're letting go of, and you gain so much more."

Pierce added, "It's like surfing." He and Garcia stood, seeming to wait for some cue.

Shay laughed and continued, "Right. While surfing, you don't use your own power. You swim hard to get away from shore, then you catch a wave and allow the immense power of the ocean to carry you. You just add the balance and your movements to tweak the course. Strengthening your muscles will help you with agility and maneuvering, but it's always, always the ocean that provides the power."

Pierce and Garcia dropped to the floor and popped up surfer style, holding their arms to the side to balance on their imaginary boards.

I groaned inwardly. *Well, I did choose not to go to a therapy group.*

"Jesus freaks," Pierce said. The Justins settled down on the floor again.

"You have all the power you need in you already from God, but you're choking it off, pushing it away. That makes you fall off your surfboard. The true you is always in alignment with Him."

I was getting uncomfortable. Were they going to ask me to get on my knees and pray with them? They were, I just knew it. Or do one of those circles where you hold hands and pray.

"We overestimate how much control we have to begin with. We can't control what others do or how they feel about us. I want you to try this." He leaned so close I could see his individual eyelashes and the darker colored specks in his irises. "Sit up straight and put your arms on your lap, with your fists closed, like this."

I sat forward some, but felt awkward, open. "Close my eyes?"

He considered. "No. Leave them open."

I looked over at the others. They seemed unsure whether they should pretend to concentrate on the bracelets or watch openly. Shay followed my glance. "Go ahead and watch. You guys will learn something here."

My face felt warm as all three joined in giving me their full attention. I looked past Shay at the wall. A travel poster of Jerusalem was curling away from its push pins. This was worse than at the store. "Now what?"

"Do you see any demons? Anywhere?"

I looked at him, then at the others. Two pairs of eyes stopped blinking as they realized I was looking for demons on them.

"No, none."

Shay spoke quietly, like a hypnotist. "Okay, relax. Look inside. Look at what it is you don't want to see, look at what you don't want to think about."

Thoughts of Chas leaped to my mind. Something I didn't want to think about. Shay stood and walked to my side. "Think about how it makes you feel, imagine it's in your fists, and then see yourself letting go of it as you open up your hands."

It flared up. The hurt, Chas's lies, his hard-heartedness, his coldness in leaving me. I thought I meant something to him, but I was just an obstacle. My face felt warm as the injustice of it burned. I tried to push it away, but there was Shay's voice, now behind me. "Open your hands and drop the weight, the pain, let it fall."

I wasn't letting it fall. I clenched my fists tighter. I "looked" at it, this seething mass inside me, and I saw flashes of Chas's behavior, his words, his facial expressions. Like a series of video clips, I saw all the interactions I had been playing over and over in my head while I tried to figure out why it all went wrong.

"El?"

"He should apologize to me. He was wrong. He hurt me. If he said he was sorry and meant it, I could forgive him and move on with my life."

From the corner of my eye I saw color and motion. I turned to the guys sitting on the floor, saw a demon on each of them, and gasped. Eyes shut tight, I hugged myself with my aching arms. "I saw them." I leaned back, felt Shay's warm body, and moved away, both embarrassed and wanting the touch to continue.

Shay stepped back but stayed near. "You saw them, demons? Are they still here? Look."

It was hard to make myself look at the guys again. They were sitting very, very still, and their eyes were wide. "No demons." With that relative feeling of relief and safety, anger flooded in again, and I turned on Shay. "What did you do? You made that happen, you made them appear again!" He put his hands up to calm me or defend his face, but I wasn't calming down. "I came to you for help and you made it worse with your stupid games."

"Eliana." Even in my anger, I noticed he said my name like he was reading poetry. "Eliana, the demons are either there or they aren't. I was just trying to find out what makes you see them."

"Pain? So don't make me feel pain!" I shouted. I wanted to yell and break things and rip the posters off the walls. It was like a tiny hole had been made in the place where I kept all the pain, and I wanted to let it all flood out on him. But I was afraid I would drown in it with him.

He went back to the coffee table and sat down, but his eyes held mine. "You have pain in you. You are human, you know, and you need to feel it in order to let it go."

"Not everyone who feels pain sees demons. What made the sight stop? The pain didn't stop."

"It's too soon for me to know. But I do know that fear closes you off to things, both good and bad. It puts up walls. Love opens you up to give and receive."

"I'm supposed to walk around all lovey-dovey and happy, just so I don't see what scares me? I did feel love! If I hadn't, I wouldn't be so hurt now."

"You said you'll feel better when you forgive the guy who hurt you, so go ahead and forgive him even if he doesn't apologize. Why let him control how you feel?"

One of his crew snorted. Garcia looked guilty when I glared at him. Shay waved at him dismissively and then leaned forward, elbows on his knees. "When you're closed off, you miss the good stuff too. You can be hurt without being destroyed. I can teach you about this, if you want to learn. Love doesn't make you stop seeing the demons. Love makes the demons irrelevant."

I stared at him. He was so weird. As if you could look at demons and say they're unimportant. And he wanted me to be willing to be hurt. No normal person would want that.

"No." I couldn't help smiling at my small rebellion.

His face remained pleasant. Maybe he didn't care whether I came back or not.

"Okay. Just be calm inside yourself. When everything is crazy around you, remember what I said about surfing. Just know that there are waves you can ride. God will bring you in to shore. Practice the visualization of letting go. If you want to come back, then next time we can work on it some more."

"You aren't giving me any 'I don't see it because it doesn't exist' mantras?"

"More like 'Yes, it's there, but I don't have to fear it because God is protecting me.'"

"But I don't see God." The Justins held their breath like they both wanted to speak, but they deferred to Shay.

"You will see him; just pay attention, and you'll learn to see."

I stretched my shoulders and picked up my purse. That's when I saw the Bryce bag, just sitting in one of the chairs with a pile of throw pillows. Shay followed my glance, and handed the perfect, luscious Bryce handbag to me.

"It seemed pretty important to you that day, so . . ."

I clutched it tightly, looking at the details of the scene on the purse as fields became mountains that became sky, then relaxed my grip to avoid creasing it. It was like being back at the store and not being able to speak. "It's for Mariah," I forced out. "She's my best friend and I wanted to give her something special."

Pierce found the store's shopping bag to put it in. I fumbled in my own purse for my wallet. I couldn't look at Shay's face. I couldn't find the words to ask why he had bought it. Helping a stranger with a medical emergency was enough, why did he stand in line for who knows how long just to do something nice for someone he didn't even know?

"I can write you a check. Or I can go to an ATM if there's one nearby." My stomach tightened at that, still feeling vulnerable about being out alone.

"It's okay, it's late. Next time."

I pulled my checkbook out. "Wait a minute." I looked at him, suspicious. "How did you even know about this time? When you bought the bag, how did you know you would ever see me again?"

His face looked tired, sad. "I knew," he said, "I often know things. You're not the only one with a gift." Shay leaned against the couch. "I usually don't tell people this, but you need to know that the supernatural does mix with the natural."

"Shay's a prophet." Pierce looked proud at this, then bent back to his bracelet at a look from Shay.

I was distracted by the realization I had used my last check at the therapist's. Maybe prophet didn't always mean what I thought it meant. "A what?"

"Just pay me back next time you see me," Shay said.

"Are you sure?" He was teasing me. Had to be.

"I trust you. Just call if you need help before then." To the others he said, "Team, time to get to work."

"Wait, wait," Pierce scrambled up and ran to me, Garcia close behind. "Wear this." He held out one of the bracelets they had made.

"Okay." I held my wrist out. Pierce hesitated when he saw the red mark above my wrist. "Go ahead." He slipped the bracelet on, and Garcia adjusted the size gently.

I thanked them and turned to go.

Shay cleared his throat and said, "Team, do you need help getting ready?"

I heard the sounds of hurried tidying as I walked to the door. When I looked back Shay waved, but his focus was on the two boys.

I walked into the hall, Shay's voice fading behind me. Those guys were freaky. Nice, but freaky. I wanted a second opinion. At the bulletin board, I slipped the Jon Addison flyer out of the trash and put it in my purse.

11

Demon Theories

I carried the flyer around in my purse, as a reminder that I had another option to explore. The hallucinations or whatever were back in full force.

Setting up my first client of the day, my stomach was tied in knots. I think he took me to be an introvert because I was looking at his shoes as much as possible. They were attractive shoes, but it was the black scaly creature pressed against his lower lip that I was trying to not see.

"Just let me know if you need anything, Mr. Scott. Can I get you a water?"

"No, I'm fine, thanks. I just ate breakfast." He smiled, and the thing held its place.

I looked at the monitor, but it wasn't visible there. As an experiment, I held up my own camera and looked through the eyepiece. No, I couldn't see it through that either. He frowned and shifted in his seat.

"Sorry, we'll get started now."

Everything went smoothly, and at the end I walked him out to the reception desk where he proceeded to eat three of the mini candy bars in the candy bowl. He put two more in his pocket. Must have had a terrible breakfast.

I had a ton of customers scheduled and had to face the fact that I would be looking at people all day. I decided to try and just suck it up. Besides, the demons didn't touch me, only "their" people. I resigned myself to the fact that this was my new normal.

I tried taking pictures of them on people and tried seeing them in mirrors—I couldn't. I tried touching them—I couldn't. One of them was on the side of a woman's head, curled around her ear. While she adjusted her nubby knit sweater and earrings, I took the opportunity to fuss with her long hair and touched her head. I only felt her hair and her skull behind her ear. But the thing reacted. It scrunched its body down and glared at me.

I had four adorable baby portrait sessions in a row. The babies, who ranged in age from two months to about two years, had no demons on them. None. Their parents did, though. Different ones, but most were on their chests, hanging on like fat little hermit crabs. Analyzing the similarities, I wondered if each type or place-ment of a demon went with a different result in the person. I made guesses about what areas they might be targeting and asked people questions about those things. Gossip was on the ear—these were the people who told me easily about coworkers stealing supplies or neighbors having affairs, while greed was on the hand; those were the people who griped about how many photos they received for how much money.

I printed out photos on autopilot while I considered all this, then slid them into large envelopes and added a sticker with the customer's name on each one. The receptionist would hand them out as customers came back at their scheduled time. Lost in my thoughts, I dropped the stack of envelopes I was carrying to the front desk. They scattered across the floor.

"Dammit." I stooped to scoop them up and slammed them into a pile. I glanced up. No customers were in the lobby. I sat on the customers' couch, dropped the envelopes onto the coffee table, and started brushing off dust as best as I could without creasing them. I hated wasting time on stupid mistakes. A flutter of panic tingled at the back of my head, which was odd, because other than the annoyance I was perfectly calm.

"Don't bend them."

It was Susan, prowling around the reception counter. Shelly must be on her break. I tried to keep my breathing steady.

"I'm not bending them. I'm being careful." My hand slipped as I dusted the bottom one, the dirtiest, and I smeared a bit of dirt into the paper envelope, staining it. Heat went from my chest to my face.

"Get a new one."

My head jerked up as I met her eyes. Of course I was going to get a clean one and fix it. *Why doesn't she tell Shelly to get the floor cleaned?* That was the real problem here.

I tried to think of something to say that would satisfy my annoyance, but not get me fired. All I could do was stare. Then I saw it. Her demon was not like the others. I had only seen them clinging to people until now. But as I watched, a black thing about the size of my thumb, like a horsefly, flew from behind her head, in a lazy circle in front of her face, then to the back of her head again.

I got off the couch and casually carried all the folders to the reception desk. I put the clean ones in the inbox for Shelly to sort when she came back from her break. I held on to the stained one and looked Susan in the eye.

"I'll take care of it Susan, don't worry."

She seemed surprised by my steady gaze. "Okay, don't forget to put a new name sticker on it. You can't reuse the old one or it will tear."

I held her gaze until she blinked rapidly and looked away from me, and a second creature joined the first. Horseflies scared me even when they were real and normal. Even without hearing the buzzing sound I expected, and knowing that they were not going to touch me, these bothered me more than any of the other demons. I was relieved they didn't follow me.

Maybe the demons avoid me because I can see them.

I walked back to the studio and fixed the portfolio, but waited until I heard Shelly return before I went out front again. Shelly dropped her purse in a drawer and closed it. A bright green creature held onto her ear, and I first mistook it for a flashy earring. Susan was nowhere in sight. I placed the portfolio in the box and leaned on the counter.

"So Shelly, what's up with Susan?"

"What do you mean?" She looked cautious.

"The way she's acting lately." As if I've known her more than a few weeks. "Is something wrong?"

Shelly bit her lip. She seemed to be in a mental battle over whether to tell me. At the end of it, she leaned forward in her seat and whispered, "It's her husband. Cancer."

That was way more than I expected. "Really?" was all that would come out.

"Well, they're still testing. I think the biopsy is tomorrow, but if it's the bad kind . . ."

"You mean malignant?"

"Yeah, it could be really serious."

"Wow, that would be scary." I did feel bad for Susan, even though I was always uncomfortable around her. She criticized everything.

The rest of the day, I snapped photos of random people I saw with demons. A woman walking through the mall with heavy shopping bags and a limp from a raw ankle where her shoe was rubbing. A man at the gas station carefully pumping only five dollars' worth of gas. Each time I was disappointed that the photos didn't give me any evidence—there was not even a shadow or blur to indicate the presence of the things clinging to them. I could still remember where the demons had been on their bodies, but the only indication of their existence was written on peoples' faces and body language. I was beginning to see the difference between a brave front and a truly happy face.

***

When I got home, it had been a long day, and chilling on the couch was what I needed. I found I wasn't missing Chas's company as much as I was just angry and hurt about the breakup. Maybe I was also jealous that he was moving forward to reach his dreams. I hadn't given up my dream, but I was a little sidetracked by circumstances. I made the decision to definitely go to Jon Addison's talk at the bookstore, and I traded a work shift with another employee to get that day off.

At the studio the next morning, I lifted a hand to wave at Susan, but she was studying the appointments book and didn't seem to see me.

My first client was an edgy businessman who needed new headshots for work. He kept readjusting his collar and cuffs. I badly wanted to brush off his face, but I knew I couldn't knock off the thin, green salamander-thing that clung close to his left eye. Its color pulsed as it moved, from light spring green to a deeper pea and back.

"You're in the oil business?"

"More or less. We do upstream work, supplying the equipment needed for exploration and drilling, not really the oil itself."

I didn't really follow that, but okay.

"What are the headshots for? Anything special?"

"No, but the others in my department have them. I want to be ready if I need them."

"That's a good idea." I said it with enthusiasm, but he wasn't in a talky mood. I posed him and distracted him from fiddling with his clothes and snapped the photos. Nothing artsy like I would prefer to be doing, but sometimes I was proud of the creative things I did retouching tricky hairlines and facial hair.

Mr. Businessman left politely but quickly and my next client came in—a girl only a year or two younger than I was. She wanted portraits, but was mysterious about what they were for. Or who they were for. She nervously set down a gym bag.

"I brought a change of clothes. I wasn't sure how much time you would have."

"The photo package you bought includes just one set of clothes." That always sounded strange, like we were giving them clothes with the photos. We weren't supposed to say "doesn't include yada yada" if at all possible. Make everything positive. She was wearing blue jeans, a plaid top over a white ribbed turtleneck, and blue suede sneakers.

She stood with her right toe possessively pressing down on the strap of the bag. She shifted her weight. "It won't take long. I just couldn't decide which thing to wear."

I smiled to put her at ease. "When that happens, it usually means that both outfits are equally fine."

She looked down at the bag again. She was pretty in an understated kind of way. Natural makeup, straight smooth hair. If my life had been a little calmer I might have invited her to do some modeling. But she was so jumpy.

Still trying to figure her out, I fiddled with the camera as if I weren't ready yet. "Can I see what you brought? It might depend on how drastic a change . . ."

She had already bent down and opened the bag. Pink fluffy ruffles pooched out like she had cut open the bag's stomach.

Why on earth? was what I wanted to ask. She'd come in with clothes that would look fine for a selfie and get her lots of likes online, but were a bit boring considering she was paying for professional portraits. On the other hand, the pink ruffly dress, which I could see in all its glory once she pulled it out of the bag, along with its matching pink bejeweled shoes, was out of place without an event to give it context.

"Um." I stared at the whole getup. "How long would it take you to change and be ready?"

"Not long."

"'Not long' means twenty minutes. I'll give you five minutes." I turned and walked out. The swishing noises told me she was changing into the dress. I can't even say it felt right to encourage her—I just did it. I poured out the rest of my coffee, which was going cold, and took a bathroom break.

I had my hand on the doorknob and was about to knock to go back into the studio. I could hear a little noise inside so I figured she was making last-minute adjustments. But I took a moment to think. I hadn't seen any demon on her yet, and I would enjoy the peace of not seeing one. But the strange girl was making me curious. That odd feeling of panic flared up and then was gone as I wondered what her demon would look like. I took a deep breath and focused on how her face had looked when I said she could wear the dress.

"Knock, knock, I'm coming in," I called through the door, then turned the doorknob. She was standing awkwardly in the middle of the room, lined up with the camera. I didn't see any demons on her as she smoothed the dress, or perhaps she was drying her palms. I gave her a big smile as I went to the camera. "Wow, that's beautiful. Turn around, let me see the back."

I only said it to get her to move and forget to be uncomfortable. I doubted the back of the dress would equal the front. But when she twirled around, I saw a demon in the middle of her shoulder blades. It was a horrible contrast to the forced sweetness of the outfit. It was black and crumbly like burnt toast. A snarling head moved from side to side on its dragonlike body, as if it were trying to regain its balance.

She completed the turn and looked at my face. "You look amazing," I said. And I meant it. She looked determined.

I only had about ten minutes before my next client. I had to be clever. I got her into a couple poses, telling her what would show off the dress so she would relax her face. I fiddled with the light to stall. "Where did you buy that dress? It must have been a specialty shop."

She frowned. "No, it was a gift."

"Oh, who from?" I was keeping it light. I'm not good at being nosey, and I felt like she was shutting down, so I had to keep pushing myself to dig deeper.

"My ex-boyfriend."

Oh good Lord, that only brought up another twenty questions. Why would any man buy or give a Pepto-Bismol Barbie doll dress . . .

"He wanted me to be a bridesmaid in his sister's wedding."

Okay, bridesmaid's dress explained a lot. I had her pose to show off her figure and the dress and started taking pictures.

"So, what happened?"

She tensed up again. "I found out it was just to antagonize his family. I wasn't . . . their kind of girl. He told them I lived out of town so they wouldn't meet me till that day. I didn't know that and looked up his sister's information online because I thought it would be weird to not meet before the wedding."

"Yeah, of course." I had her swirl around to show the back while she looked off to one side. I stepped away quickly as the dragon-thing gripped harder onto her back and snarled at me again.

"He used me. And now I hate him. But I'm wearing the dress, just to show him."

I snapped some more photos while she had that look of cold anger in her eyes. Standing there without the context of a wedding to make her outfit sensible, she emanated strength.

When her time was up, I walked her to the ladies room, where she could change while I set up for my next client. "If he rejects your emails or messages, we can send the photos from here. Just let me know." Her shocked look was the last thing I saw as the door closed. But I understood the revenge thing, and I wanted to help her.

12

Bookstore

Saturday morning, the sun was bright in a cloudless sky. In the ritzy part of town, I pulled into a palm-tree-lined parking lot and decided to keep the sunglasses on. But as I entered the immense bookstore, the tinted windows blocked the glare and the fluorescents took over, so I packed the sunnies away. I hadn't seen any demons that morning, but my gut told me I wasn't through this yet.

The night I went to the church, once I had gotten home safely, thank God, I looked more closely at the flyer from the church bulletin board. I didn't know what to think of the graphic on it: a woman in a Jane Austen-era dress being handed a small treasure chest of jewels by a mournful-looking angel with a broken wing. It advertised a speaking engagement by Jon Addison and promised to make your dreams come true. I had smoothed out the crumpled lines and rips at the corners where Shay had torn it off the wall. And who had written *"demons"* across it? Shay?

The bookstore was quietly busy. A sign near the stairs pointed the way up to the Loft Lounge, a multipurpose space for book signings and kids' activities. I walked up as nonchalantly as I could, expecting hippies and crystal-wielding New Agers to be gathered. The people looked pretty much like me, but better dressed—especially the women. There were a lot of women.

I was still a little ticked off at Shay. He could be cocky. Arguing with someone who kept smiling was annoying. And he had put his card in the Bryce with the receipt. It was a simple white card with black lettering with his name, address, and cell number. A Bible verse was handwritten on the back. I did stick the card in my purse—maybe I would mail a check for payment to his house. I kept putting it off because I *could* just drop it off at the church.

I drifted around the bookstore loft, near where the employees were setting up a podium and long table with one chair and a stack of . . . not books, but boxes with the angel design on the front. The children's section was nearby, so I looked through the Dr. Seuss books just for fun. From what the employees were saying to each other, I gathered that Jon did these events a few times per year.

Five minutes before the signing was due to start, people settled into the rows of chairs. Several women in the front row seemed to know each other from previous Jon Addison events. They were attractively put together for a chilly Saturday morning. I picked a seat in the middle of the next to last row, stepping carefully over the legs of a bored-looking man with a drooping gray mustache.

When I looked up again, a man in his early twenties wearing a trendily cut, medium blue suit was whispering with the event manager and straightening the items on the signing table. Yes, a suit. He looked like he was about to run his hand across his light scruff of a beard and pose for a catalog shoot. *OMG, why did I leave the camera in the car?*

With a final glance around the room, he stepped up to the low podium. "Good morning, I am Jon Addison, writer, lecturer, and opportunist." The audience laughed as he beamed at them. He made eye contact with a few people, acknowledging them with a nod.

That's really him? I was expecting some old college professor covered in chalk dust and carrying cloudy bottles of medicinal plants. He was supposed to have a thin, reedy voice, not be hunk man.

"Not that long ago, I was working at a successful real estate office. The clients were successful business people. Intelligent, hardworking people who were still looking for 'luck.' They wanted to feng shui their house to get it to sell or to have some talisman or ritual that would work in their favor. In working with them, I realized even reasonable people love to put their fate in the hands of someone or something else. Putting themselves in the hands of a realtor wasn't good enough, apparently." He paused for the audience's laughter. "No, they wanted supernatural help.

"What about prayer? What about God? Most people are reluctant to ask the Almighty to stoop to the level of getting them a few thousand dollars more for the slipshod kitchen upgrade they did to sell the house.

"Then let's take a step down from God. Angels. They were created to serve, and many believe we each have a guardian angel assigned to look after us. Still, people are reluctant to ask angels for worldly goods. We feel like we shouldn't want those things, and it is vulgar to ask Heavenly beings for them. The problem is we need food, clothes, housing . . . *money* to survive in our society. Need them, and we do want them."

Jon's eyes met mine. I held my breath. *Does he know? Can he see there is something about me?* He moved on, locking eyes with various people in the room. I realized I was leaning forward in my chair to catch his every word. I forced myself to relax back; this could still be another dead-end, and I didn't want to get my hopes up too soon. He looked back at me once more and smiled as he went on.

"There is another group of angels without those lofty concerns. They were made to serve like all other angels, but they turned their back on the higher things. And yet we can still get the help of these more 'worldly' angels. But how?

"That's where I come in. I have done extensive research on this problem, and I have found the way to connect you with supernatural beings eager to supply you with the things of the world that your soul longs for. And you don't even have to read a book to do it." Laughter emanated from the audience again. "My *Worldly Angels Ultimate Service Kit* contains a DVD of yours truly explaining the process, a CD with guided meditations to connect you to your 'helpers,' a brief booklet in case you must have reading material"—giggles from the front row—"and a charm to wear to remind you of the help that is available for you."

He paused here, lifting one hand from the podium and reaching toward us.

"You live in the world and need only reach out your hand to have the things of the world. Your helpers simply extend your reach."

He didn't have a book signing exactly, since it wasn't a book. And no question and answer session. Only people who bought the kit could go through the line to speak to him. He was sweet and unflappable, but anyone questioning his theory or theology was urged by bookstore employees to step aside for the next person.

Worldly Angels came in either the *Basic* or *Ultimate Service Kit*. I picked the kit up and put it down five times. I started to worry they'd think I was shoplifting. Or worse, that he'd think I was waiting to flirt with him like the four women from the front row who were now hanging around the top of the stairs in a vigilant knot. The feeling of dread was made worse because he was handsome and seemed so sweet. I didn't want him to get the wrong idea and think I was a groupie.

"Did you have any questions I could help you with?"

Great, the store employees had noticed me.

"I'm just look . . ."

I trailed off when I looked up into a pair of sparkly blue eyes. Jon smiled down at me. "I can open a box if you want a closer look."

Tongue-tied, I watched as he deftly opened the kit. It unfolded to display the DVD, CD, booklet, and on top, a tiny angel charm. I bent to look closer. The angel was silver with red wings. One of the wings stood out from its body in a graceful arc. The other wing, though still visible behind the angel's back, showed a distinct break at the top. I got a weird feeling in the pit of my stomach as I looked at the broken-winged angel. I wanted very much to buy the kit, though I was no longer sure if it was to learn about the "helpers" or the appeal of the warm voice in my ear.

"You can wear it around your neck or keep it on your purse or backpack."

A feeling of dread welled up inside me, telling me to shove the thing away and leave as fast as possible.

Jon reached out his hand. "Jon Addison."

Weakly, I shook it. "Eliana Williams."

"Nice to meet you, Eliana."

I was glad it was cold enough to wear long sleeves. The man who grabbed me the other night had left bruises on my arms, but my shirt covered them. I self-consciously touched the scratches I had put on the side of my own neck.

"Nice to meet you too. I should go." That was good. No fake explanation or it would just trail off into obvious um . . . fakeness. His eyes were perfect, and he had smooth skin, with just enough of a tan to look relaxed and outdoorsy, and just enough self-confidence to look knowledgeable.

"I was going to get some coffee. Would you like to join me?"

A date? Was he asking me on a date? Perhaps he could see that I was unusual, and if he saw that, maybe he knew how to help me. An employee interrupted, covering my new wave of speechlessness.

"Is there anything else we can get you, Mr. Addison?" She stood a little too close as she looked up at him, her bookstore uniform unbuttoned one too low.

He flashed his perfect smile at her. "No thank you, Jennifer, I'm ready to go." She shot a quick look at me and turned away. The front-row women still hovered. Store employees had finished putting away the extra kits and were stacking the chairs.

Jon picked up his coat and tilted his head toward the waiting women. "I could get out of here faster if you would accompany me to the front door. I don't want to be rude to them, but there's nothing they can ask that I haven't already answered."

I held back a laugh. Oh, the problems of the beautiful and famous. Was he famous? I wondered. "Okay, I'll follow your lead." I had an immediate surge of stage fright over this simple thing, but I needn't have worried. Jon waved at the women as we walked to the top of the stairs, but otherwise he kept up a nonstop monologue to me on coffee, bookstores, and the weather all the way to the front door of the store.

Outside, he offered his hand again with a slight bow. "So nice to meet you, Miss Eliana. Thank you for rescuing me."

My head swam. I wanted to be funny, but a remark about his groupies might sound catty. "Happy to be your knight in shining armor, or princess I guess." *What?*

He laughed. Then hesitated. "The coffee is still an option, if you would like. There's a place on the other side of the parking lot that isn't bad."

Yes and no both came to my lips. I controlled myself and scrutinized his face. I still had so many questions.

"Coffee sounds good."

13

Coffee

The coffeehouse was buzzing with aspiring novelists tapping away on laptops and hipster baristas discussing their dates from last night. The decor tried a little too hard, but at least the music was quiet enough to talk over. Big plastic stick-on snowflakes decorated the window by our table. Snow was rare in Houston, but it did serve as a holiday decoration like in the rest of the US. We had our coffees and a cookie, cut into four slices to share.

"What brought you to the event today?" His smile was warmer and less showy than when he was at the podium.

"Uh . . ." I wasn't ready to talk about my "visions" yet again. I wanted help or at least hope, but it's frustrating to pour your heart out over and over and not get anywhere. Before I told him, I wanted to be sure he wasn't just a huckster. My mind went to the flyer in my purse.

"Oh, I saw a notice on a bulletin board."

"Great. Where was that?"

"The River of Hope Church."

Something like a smirk crossed his face, but then he smiled. "Ah, you go to River of Hope, that's a good church."

"I don't go—well, I went Wednesday to ask about . . ." I loosened the death grip I had on my coffee mug. Pressing my damp palms on the table, I took a deep breath and asked, "Jon, do you believe that demons exist in the modern world?"

Without hesitation he said, "Of course. They were brazen enough to wander in Israel when the Son of God was walking the Earth, so why wouldn't they be running rampant now?"

I decided to open up. A little. "I've been having nightmares about . . . um . . . supernatural beings."

"Demons, I guess, since you asked about them. That would be scary."

"It is. I wondered if you, you know, knew how to make them stop."

"Well, I don't deal with demons." He pinched his lower lip as he looked out the window. "Not exactly." I was able to study his face better while he looked away, but try as I might, I couldn't pin down his age. His work experience pointed to someone much older, but his face didn't fit.

He took a breath and said, "And they're just dreams . . . maybe you're under stress?" He looked at me for confirmation, but I didn't give it. "People who buy my kits are just getting a little help, a nudge, toward what they want to do anyway. When they have an issue, their helper makes them feel like they have an ally." He pushed the cookie plate toward me. "Did the people at the church answer your questions? I've met their pastor. He seems nice."

I broke off a small bite of cookie. "I guess I didn't get the answer I wanted, which is how to make it stop and be normal again. I met a few people in a group . . ." I struggled to remember the names from the spiritual gifts group, but couldn't. "And I met some teenagers."

"Shay?" he asked with a grin.

"Yeah, I met Shay."

"Shay is one of a kind. Quite enthusiastic. It was a blow to him, what happened to his girlfriend. Did he tell you?"

"No, he didn't say anything about a girlfriend." Jon kept looking at me. I went on, "He talked about love, being open . . ." I couldn't say the rest—being open to being hurt. Tears started welling in my eyes.

Jon covered my hand with his. "Hey, are you okay? Did he upset you?" He grabbed a napkin and held it out for me. I dabbed my eyes, though I was reluctant to pull away from the comfort of that one touch.

"No, I . . . I had a bad experience this week—that night that I went to the church . . ." Jon's look turned angry, like he was going to run out and fix whoever had hurt me. "I was walking at night, at—" I didn't want to say I had been to therapy. "In an area I don't know well, and a man grabbed me." Jon handed me more napkins, as my tears were coming faster now. "He tried to push me into his car. I was so scared. A homeless man came up and saved me. If he hadn't, I might . . . I don't know if . . ."

I had told the police and I had told Mariah just the bare bones of it. It hadn't gotten any less frightening, though. Just the idea of being robbed or hit had already been enough to scare me into checking my surroundings repeatedly every time I went outside. But knowing I could be dead or getting rape counseling now made me nauseous.

Jon patted my arm. "You're okay. You're safe now." I winced as he gave my arm a gentle squeeze. "I'm sorry." He jerked both hands back. "I didn't . . ."

"No," I said, voice still wavering, "it's not you." I wanted the comfort. The only way I could explain was to yank my sleeve up as high as it would go. The bruise he touched was still purple. "It's where he grabbed me. I have a few others. It's still sore."

Jon's face got a tinge of purple as he glared at my arm. "Eliana, I'm so sorry. Did the police get him?"

"No." I pulled the sleeve back down. "I couldn't give them much info."

He met my eyes. "He should pay for that. I believe the police will find him." He gave my hand a clumsy pat. "Don't worry."

We sat in silence for several minutes. It was comforting, not awkward. "Thank you," I said at last, "I feel better. I should go, though. Thanks for the coffee."

He waved away my thanks. "I'm sorry I brought up something upsetting for you." It was my turn to wave it away dismissively.

We walked back across the parking lot together. It had turned out to be a beautiful day, the afternoon promised to be almost spring-like.

We stopped by my car. I shifted so his body blocked the glare that was glinting off the windshield of a black Lexus nearby. "Thanks Jon, it was nice talking to you."

"Likewise," he said. "Maybe we could talk again. Can I have your phone number?"

I felt a little giddy, but kept it to myself. We traded phones to exchange phone numbers. I hate when people are startled that it's not a smart phone, like I pulled an old rotary phone out of my pocket, cord and all, but Jon was cool about it.

He smiled, and his hand felt warm as we handed our phones back. As I got into my car, he climbed into the Lexus and revved it up. I watched as he pulled out. His vanity plate read *"MOVINUP."*

14

Catching Up With Mariah

Jon and I texted every day. The soft drip sound of my phone gave me random surprises, like little presents to open. Famous quotes, a photo of a bird outside his window, an occasional rant about something. I never knew what it would be. In turn, I sent him lots of photos of the mall—it was where I spent the most time. Some of them were really good though, like the one of the little girl who fell asleep standing in line to see Santa, arms dangling, her back arching as she leaned back against her mom.

One day he texted, *"I was so upset to hear about your assault. I asked one of my associates if they know anyone who could lend a hand. They will look into it."*

I figured it was just one of those things "associates" say to get you off their back. But it was nice of him to try.

A few days later, he called as I was finishing a work shift.

"I have a meeting about a possible project this afternoon, but I'm free this evening. Do you have plans?"

"Not yet. I usually go to Dickens on the Strand and take pictures. I was debating whether to go this year."

"Oh, you should, the weather is great. If you want to talk some more, maybe we could meet after you're finished? With dinner, if you don't mind. I'll be hungry by then."

It hit me that he was asking me to go out. With him. Like a date, not just coffee. I guess I had known I would start dating again someday, and to do that I had to have a "first date since the breakup." But my mouth became dry, and I felt my defenses go up. I didn't know whether to put him off or leave it open for him. I wasn't sure I was ready.

Like he knew what I was thinking, Jon's voice sounded warm when he said, "Not everything I do is connected with the supernatural. The point of the worldly angels is to get the things you need so you can enjoy your life."

Enjoying life. I made a choice without thinking too much. I gritted my teeth as I pushed away from my comfort zone and said, "Sure, I'd like to join you."

"My meeting should be done late afternoon. What if we meet at The Black Crow at seven? You know where it is?"

"Okay. Yes, downtown." If it were a public place, it wouldn't matter that I didn't know him well. I would be safe in the crowd. I was already debating what to wear as I disconnected the call and packed up my work things.

***

I drove back to Mariah's—it still felt odd to call it home—and picked out some clothes for the evening. A long-sleeved black blouse, dark blue jeans, and short leather boots. I found some leftover baked chicken in the fridge to tide me over till dinner.

I checked my batteries and got my camera ready. I decided not to do Dickens on the Strand, because I would have to drive all the way to Galveston, then deal with traffic and parking. I still had plenty of photos from last year of people walking around in their 1800s-style costumes, so I didn't need more. I told myself I would just take some photos downtown on my way to the restaurant, hang out with this guy in public, ask him some more questions, and go home. Nice and easy.

Mariah had been juggling final exams and helping her foster mom decorate, causing us to not be home at the same time much unless one of us was asleep. It was hard to discuss personal things at the mall with other people around. I had given her the bare minimum of info on the assault. She had listened and hugged me and promised to stay home with me at night if I was afraid. I assured her I was fine. It hadn't seemed like the right time then to chat about Shay and Jon, but I *had* to talk about these guys to her. I tried to think of a way to tell her without mentioning the demons, but it would be too weird. "Oh yeah, so after my scary incident I went to a church for no particular reason, then I went to a bookstore and just happened to go out for coffee with a guy I met there." Well, that part didn't sound so weird, except it's not like me.

I was in the bathroom brushing my teeth and deciding whether to put my hair up when I heard her come in the front door. A minute later I heard her off-key rendition of "White Christmas." I dabbed my mouth to avoid wiping off my foundation and went out to see her on the floor in front of our small tree, surrounded by assorted Christmas tree decorations.

"El, why did you buy so many icicles?" Mariah held up four slim boxes of tinsel strands, then looked at my face. "Oh my God, you're wearing makeup? Where are you going?"

My face felt warm and I hoped it wouldn't cause anything to run. "I'm going out later." I pointed at the icicles as I sat on the couch. "Is that a lot?" They're just slivers of metallic foil, it's not like I knew how many strands per square foot of tree or anything. "Mom doesn't like them, so I don't get to put them on at home."

"Keep your receipt, and you can take back any excess."

Better not tell her about the three packages of exterior twinkle lights that I had already opened.

Decorating the small tree should have taken about five minutes, but we kept rearranging ornaments. We merged what she had traditionally done at home with what I wanted to try out. I thought the white ones would be too plain, but they had an iridescent shine. I added the armadillo in a cowboy hat ornament I had found at the mall and my excessive icicles. I started to wonder if Mom's no icicle rule came from the fact that the darn things were hard to handle. They stuck to my fingers, not the tree. Then, when I tried to re-arrange them on the tree, they didn't cooperate with that either.

"I was going to ask if you want to watch a Christmas movie tonight, but it looks like you have plans. And I'm not trying to keep tabs on you—I'm just curious," she added, looking worried.

"I don't mind. I like knowing someone is looking out for me." I grinned. Pity the fool that hurts one of Mariah's loved ones. "I have to leave soon, and I still need to tell you about the guys."

Mariah stopped short. "Guys, plural?"

"Yeah, plural," I said. "Last week I went to a church to see about their group counseling, and I ran into the guy from the mall who helped me during—well, you remember Shay." I was still uncom-fortable talking about the incident. "And then a few days later, I met Jon at a bookstore. He's an author, and I had coffee with him after his event. I'm going to see him again this evening."

"Can I see the book?"

"It's more of a DVD package, and I didn't buy it."

"Oh, well, that's cool though, an author. And he must like you, he didn't waste any time asking you out."

I laughed, then stopped. I hadn't met either of them with the intention of dating. And Jon had said Shay had a girlfriend, but their relationship could be history by now. Maybe one part of my brain had considered dating, because they were both . . .

"Hello?"

"I was just thinking, they're both attractive, but I didn't really view them like that. I want whatever help each of them can give me with this . . . problem. Shay is some kind of gung-ho church addict, and bookstore guy sells a program to match you with a supernatural helper kind of thing."

She wrinkled her nose.

"No, he seems cool." I sat back, rolling stray icicles in my sweaty palms. "Jon is handsome in an older guy kind of way. He's about early to mid-twenties, but he acts like . . . I dunno . . . thirty-five? All capable and mature and successful, but smoldering underneath."

"A grown-up."

I laughed for real at that. "Yes, he's a man! And he does research on these, um, angelic beings . . ."

"He researches angels?"

"Uh, no. More like fallen angels." She arched her brows at that. "Anyway, he takes me seriously about seeing—well, I only told him I have nightmares about demons." I pushed some stray hairs off my neck into my hair clip. "Shay is . . . well he's hot too, just in a different way. He's a little too intense, but kind at the same time. And Shay seems to hate Jon. I don't know why yet."

I watched her twist tree branches into perfect balance with each other. Her little chest clawer of a demon appeared. I shut my eyes and tried to focus on what I was saying. "Maybe I'll ask him what his problem is with Jon, I still have to pay him . . ." Oh shoot, I didn't want her to know about the purse. My brain struggled to find a cover-up. When I opened my eyes again, the demon was gone.

Mariah was still rearranging ornaments on the tree. "You don't have to pay him back, El. He was just being a decent person when you had your seizure." I breathed a sigh of relief.

"I guess it's not a big deal. If anything develops with either one later on, after I'm cured, it's not like we would all be hanging out together anyway."

Mariah tossed an icicle onto my head. "Almost done." She dashed to her bedroom. I sized up the tree. Not bad. It might have been a little better with just the simple ornaments—more elegant. It didn't need the glitz of the icicles, even though they did fill in that one bare spot where a plastic tree limb was missing. Mariah returned with two items and a stern face. "Not one word," she cautioned me.

She placed the gold-painted popsicle stick birdcage I had made for her under the tree. Next she picked up the bracelet I had made for another past Christmas gift. She looped it in the needles so its small star charm hung at the top of the tree. "Perfect," she said proudly.

I had actually worked hard on those gifts, so I nodded and said, "Yes, it's perfect."

15

The Black Crow

Downtown was beautiful. Lights decorated most of the office buildings. In previous years, dips in the economy had made decorations sparse, but the big companies were getting back to throwing some money around, and the effect was magical.

I stood at an intersection surrounded by a swirl of people. I always felt most comfortable in crowds with my camera in my hand. It wasn't just that photography gave me a reason to be out and interacting with people, but it also formed an invisible wall between me and my subjects, as if I were already looking at them on a computer screen.

I still had a little time before I was supposed to meet Jon at the restaurant, and I came across a group of carolers on the sidewalk. Their singing was beautiful. Lights twinkled behind them. I took a few pictures, then Jon appeared at my elbow. He wore a long black wool coat. There's something sexy about a man in a long coat. He presented me with a wrist corsage. It was cute. Nothing showy, just two pretty pink rosebuds that I didn't have to carry around in my hands.

I was surprised to feel myself relax. It only took two songs for me to stop plotting the best vantage points if I were shooting the event professionally. Other than one quick thought of how annoying it would be to see demons on every person in this crowd, I didn't even give them a thought. Jon was part of the reason; he looked after me and made sure no one tall stood in front of me. But he also didn't try to upstage the performance or keep my attention on him. He let me be.

The cold was just starting to get to me when the last song ended. Jon led me to The Black Crow. He only touched me when he needed to guide my direction on the crowded sidewalk.

Inside the restaurant, red and black dominated the decor. Cushy chairs and Victorian lampshades set the tone in the bar area, while people without reservations clustered in the entryway. Jon gestured for me to follow the hostess to a cozy booth near the back. It had been too busy on the street to talk, so we settled in and chatted about the carolers and the Christmas lights. While he clicked through the photos on my camera, I took a good look around.

The Black Crow was a quaint pub with sturdy wood banisters, tapestries on the wall, and an abundance of beers on tap. The theme was horror movies. Over the tables hung props hinting at stories of vampires, werewolves, and serial killers. Our booth was a little simpler, with only a modest painting of priests at the bedside of a dying man. He seemed to be dying in agony, and was holding an arm out—warning or pleading, I don't know.

I skimmed through the menu. They offered basic pub grub with a few clever horror movie names. The waitress brought our drinks. Jon was quite the caffeine junkie; he had a large coffee.

"I have news, El. I wanted to tell you in person." He looked eager.

"Oh?" I put down the menu.

"I asked my associate for an update on your case. The police found the guy. Dead."

I shivered, head to toe. "I don't believe it." I was relieved, but cautious. "How could they, or your friend, even know it's the same guy?"

Jon put his hand over his mouth like he was hiding a smile, then got serious. "He was a serial rapist, operating in the neighborhood you were in. The details of your case, the way he operated, matched the other cases, except that you got away. You don't have to be afraid anymore."

That one man, horrible as he was, wasn't what had kept me awake at night. What I had was more of a general fear of running into another random attacker. And even that was less than the revulsion I felt at seeing demons on people. My main fears in the past had been rapists, grizzly bears, being abandoned, and fire ants. More or less in that order. Now demon visions topped the list.

"But he's dead? How?"

Jon shrugged and opened his menu. "He was found in an alley. Some violent cause of death. Everything has a price." He flipped a couple pages. "I told you I knew influential people." He looked up at my still-dumbfounded expression. "But that's what you wanted, right? For him to be gone?"

I looked down at my drink napkin and realized I was ripping it into pieces. "What I want is to be normal again and stop seeing demons everywhere—I mean, in my sleep." China clattered, and I looked up.

Jon's expression remained unreadable as he rearranged his coffee cup, wiped up a coffee puddle on the table, folded the dirty napkin, then cleared his throat. "What have you tried so far?"

"Doctors, therapy, affirmations, church meeting groups, Shay and his 'team' . . ."

"Shay, of course. He would be the church's resident expert on demons. After what happened to his girlfriend and all."

Expert? Shay didn't say anything about actual experience with demons.

"You mentioned his girlfriend before. What happened to her?"

Jon frowned and fidgeted with his coffee spoon. "It was a bad situation all round. She was committed to an institution. She had started seeing . . . things, and had no one to help her until her condition worsened." He met my gaze. "Shay was in denial about it, saying she was fine and didn't need help. It really tore him up. He's so devoted to her."

"Wait, so you go to that church too? You know them all—the Justins and everyone?"

He laughed. "No, I work at the psychiatric hospital that Rose, his girlfriend, is at."

My head was spinning. "I thought you said you worked in real estate?"

"I did. While I was putting myself through school."

"You're a doctor now?"

"No," he chuckled, "a medical technician. It's still not my dream job, but it's taught me a lot about thinking outside the box. Just as our minds are invisible when we look at our bodies, the invisible spirit world exists alongside the material world. Exists and interacts with it." He leaned forward. I could smell just a whiff of his cologne. "I sense that you know more about this than you're telling me, and that's fine. Let's choose some food."

We agreed on potato skins for appetizers followed by fish and chips for me and a steak, rare, for him. I realized I was getting touchy about people I didn't even know. Sure he mentioned a real estate job in his bookstore spiel, but he never said he was giving his life's story. And why should I be bothered if Shay had a girlfriend? So, we chatted about other things—Mariah, my current and past jobs, and what first date would be complete without discussing music preferences?

"What is your dream job?" I asked him.

He looked shy, but answered, "I actually took a step closer to it today. I had a meeting with a production team. We're looking into doing a video, maybe just a short documentary to start with, but my associates say it's going to expand my business tenfold. I owe them so much."

"The worldly angel business?"

He laughed. "Yes, that. We're shooting it on Christmas Eve, since one of the people I want to interview will be available then. You can come too, if you want. My partners even suggested it."

His eyelashes outlined eyes that were already drawing me in. "What? Why would they suggest it?"

"I told them I couldn't stay late at the meeting because I had a date. They said why not invite you to the taping." He laughed. "I don't know why either. I will talk about what I do and have some guests on camera to demonstrate sensitivity to paranormal vibrations." He wrinkled his nose as he smiled as if he were a little embarrassed by his side gig.

I squirmed in my seat. "Jon, I'm not interested in being on camera. It's not like I'm proud of this or anything. I just want it gone."

"I understand." He nodded, then looked . . . sad? "Everything has its . . . well, the more information we can get, the more viewpoints we can offer, the better it is for people trying to understand these phenomena." He sighed. "And I don't know if you are what they had in mind anyway. If you are just having bad dreams, those could stop at any time, right?"

Well, shoot. I did hide the full truth from him, didn't I?

I gathered my thoughts. "Jon, I didn't tell you all of it before. I was worried you would think I was crazy or just looking for attention." I glanced up at him and thought his face seemed strained. Not in a stressed way, more like he was holding in joy. Odd. He smoothed his face and nodded for me to continue. "It is more than just the dreams," I admitted. He raised his eyebrows. "I see demons on people. Not all the time, it comes and goes." I had his full attention now. Our waitress came back, but he waved her away. I leaned closer. "I . . . I think it sounds crazy myself, but I think I can see different kinds for different people—gossip or gluttony or anger . . ."

"Maybe it could be useful."

"I don't want it." I took a breath and told him about the seizure, the visions, how they meshed with the nightmares. "I'm not seeing them right now, but I wanted . . ." I looked around the room as I struggled for words; what did I want? An image of Shay flashed in my mind. I pushed it away. "I want to make them stop completely. I thought maybe you could give me advice."

Tears were threatening to well up. I was determined that I wouldn't cry in front of him again and looked away, trying to focus on anything else. I was startled to feel a touch on my hand. I looked at him again.

"El, it's okay." He held my hand more firmly. "You're okay. Take a breath." I did, a ragged one, and he went on. "This is obviously hard for you. I can help you, just know that you are not alone."

His confidence was contagious and calmed me. I debated whether escaping to the ladies' room to dab my eyes would be more awkward than staying and trying to pretend I was fine. With a final pat on my hand, he said, "I'll get our waitress back."

He disappeared while I tidied my nose and face, and reappeared with the waitress happily tagging along. She kept her eyes glued to him while he ordered for both of us with minor input from me.

Once that was done, he played with the drink menu and said, "One thing that would make it all very easy for you is to be hypnotized."

I didn't like the sound of that. I thought of hypnotism as either a magician's trick or for serious therapy—neither of which I wanted to take part in. I looked at his blue eyes and his rolled-up white sleeves and the newly shaved skin of his face that looked so touchable. I wanted to trust him.

"I know," he said. The shy look was back. "It doesn't sound appealing. You don't have to do anything you don't want to. But I'm sure I can find a way to help you."

I felt my body relax as I exhaled. Our waitress reappeared with two margaritas, one virgin and one not. Jon smiled at me. "Their margaritas are excellent. You don't have to drink it if you don't want it."

I took a sip. He was fun, just a more sedate kind of fun than Shay. I let my guard down and enjoyed his conversation. Besides, why be so cautious with him? I didn't have to worry that he would think I was crazy or brain damaged. He just saw my problem as an interesting case.

Our appetizers slid onto the table. I let Jon handle the niceties with the server. The food was as good as he had promised, and the rest of our conversation was light. By the time the check came I had put the corsage in my hair as a whimsical hair clip.

16

Service at the Park

Sunday morning—well, midmorning—I dragged myself out of bed and showered. I wanted to give Shay the purse money and get it over with. Maybe go back to sleep. I also needed to tell him that I had found someone else who could help me with the demons, so I didn't need to see him anymore. I was uncomfortable with that part.

I assumed I would find Shay at the church even after the service. I walked directly to the youth room I had visited before, but it was empty. A Sunday School teacher with an armload of art supplies and cookie boxes pointed me toward the "new" youth room. Inside, two camps were on opposite sides—high schoolers watching a movie, and middle schoolers playing video games. I didn't see Shay or his friends.

An adult volunteer checked on me as I was leaving. When I asked, he said, "Oh, Shay is working with a church service for the homeless in a park near downtown."

His card was at the bottom of my purse. I dialed the number, not sure what I was going to say.

"Hello?"

"Um, hi. I . . . this is Eliana."

"Eliana, how are you and your imaginary friends?"

"Not funny. And I'm sleepy. Where are you? I just need to pay . . ."

"COME JOIN UUUUSSSS!" A chorus of male teen voices nearly burst my eardrum. The sound of a struggle for the phone followed. The winner said, "Eliana! Ow! It's like a party in the park. Ow, Shay, let go! You gotta come here now!"

I sighed, standing there in the church hallway, holding the phone away from my ear.

Another struggle ensued on the other end of the phone.

"Hey, El." Shay's smooth voice took over. "We're serving food to homeless people in the park after an outdoor church service. I'd love it if you would come out and volunteer with us."

He said "I'd" love it. Not "we." Hmm.

"Where?"

He gave me directions and said they'd come find me if I got lost.

"Oh, and . . . Eliana?"

"Yes?"

"Leave your camera in the car."

"Um, why?"

"To be fully present. No filters."

***

I felt self-conscious as soon as I arrived at the park. I didn't know what to do with my hands. The camera would have helped. I tried to look like I knew where I was going and slowly walked toward the picnic tables. I hadn't gone ten steps before Justin and Justin came tearing toward me like a cattle stampede.

"Eliana!"

I froze, hoping they weren't going to tackle me. They skidded to a stop on the pavement, sending up a spray of dust. "We're so glad you came," said Justin One, who I think was Pierce.

A third teen, closer to my age, ran up behind them and stuck his hand out to me. "Hey Eliana, nice to meet you, I'm Dylan."

"Come with us, hurry," Justin Two grabbed my other hand, and they pulled me along. I resisted running, but they dragged me fast enough to get me breathing hard. As soon as we were clear of the cars in the parking lot, I could see Shay sitting on top of a picnic table, shielding his eyes with his hand like he was embarrassed by what he saw.

Giving food to the homeless was not what I thought. I had expected we would be walking around with bags of sandwiches, trying to get strangers to take them. But this was a thoroughly organized system from the setup to the church service to the lunch service. The worship service had already started when I arrived, so we stood at the back, singing hymns from the lyric sheets passed out by two other volunteers. I sang just above a whisper, so no one would hear my less-than-perfect pitch. I shouldn't have worried. Shay, Dylan, and the Justins sang loud and proud at . . . well, their rather joyful level of ability.

Being at the back let us slip out early to get to our places in the food serving line. Two long white folding tables were waiting with trays of hot food, steam slipping out of the edges of their lids.

"Shay, I don't have any training in this stuff. I don't know how to talk to people in this situation. What if I say something stupid?"

"Eliana, you don't have to learn how to love people. It just comes naturally."

I had my doubts, but I kept them to myself.

Shay found a baseball cap for me to wear in lieu of a hairnet, and had the woman in charge assign me a place next to him.

The men and women participating knew the routine and filed through in an orderly fashion. Shay greeted each person like an old friend as he served them ladles of chicken à la king. Garbed with plastic gloves, it was my job to add a roll to each plate. Most of the people in line went out of their way to be friendly to me, and I soon relaxed. By the end, I was watching out for the quiet ones, to be sure I greeted them and talked with them.

After the food was gone, the group of us made short work of the cleanup. That morning I had planned to tell Shay that I found someone else to help me, and this would be goodbye to him and all the weirdness. I went off to the side to get the check from my purse. Shay followed me.

"We all carpooled with Dylan today. We're leaving now. He needs to get the Justins home." He held out his hand to shake mine. "Until next time."

"Already?" I jammed the check back into my purse. "I can drive you, save him some time." My mouth felt dry.

"You don't mind?"

"Of course not." I felt awkward again, but I was off today and had nothing urgent to do. I waited while he said goodbye and hugged the minister and various volunteers. He fist-bumped his friends and walked with me toward the parking lot. Once I was alone with Shay, I didn't want to say anything about Jon.

As we walked, my mind kept going back to the service I had just taken part in.

"Shay, answer me this, if you keep feeding them, and they keep living on the street, then what is the point? I mean, you are helping them day to day, but what kind of life is that?" My face started to feel hot. I didn't want to sound cruel; I just wanted to understand what they were doing. "Does it help them get off the street? That's what you really want, right?"

"The opposite of love is not hate, it's indifference."

"Huh?"

"What would you do if someone said he wasn't going to get off the street? Say 'Well, I'm not feeding you anymore'? They don't do this for the fun of it." Shay kept the same calm, blissful smile the whole time he talked. He shut his eyes halfway against a breeze blowing his hair back off his forehead, then turned to me. "Sometimes you just have to do what is right in the moment. You can't see the future and know what is best for each person, so you just take care of them here and now. That keeps it simple." His smile grew.

"But can't you see the future? Your friends said you're a prophet." I was teasing him. I assumed it was some kind of inside joke they had.

"Not anymore."

"Why not? Lose your license?"

He stopped and looked me straight in the eye for a long moment. "I didn't do what I was told to do. By God. I disobeyed God."

"Uh huh." I stared straight back at him and realized he was serious.

He looked away and continued walking. He spoke quickly. "God told me to give a message to . . . well, an important message."

"Okay." No sarcasm.

"He said to write down what I was told and to tell it to . . . someone. But I didn't do it, and now I don't remember the message or who it was going to."

"Seriously? But that's so huge. I mean, how . . . how could you possibly forget what God said to you?"

He gave me a pained look. "I guess it's my punishment. Jonah didn't do what he was told, and he was swallowed by a whale. I had the most important moment of my life wiped from my memory."

"But maybe it's still in there. Maybe you could be hypnotized . . ."

He grabbed a hefty branch from the ground and heaved it at a tree trunk we were walking past. It made a solid *thunk* and bounced off. His voice was bitter. "It's just gone, Eliana. I can't fix it."

He walked ahead of me and over to a water fountain by the path. My brow was so wrinkled as I watched him that I made a mental note to give myself a facial soon; this guy was going to make me age faster. But why would he react like that? As I thought it, I felt that familiar, small, panicky feeling in the back of my head. For the first time, it didn't really feel like a part of me, but more like a squirrel darting out of my path.

The demons appeared. Shay had uncountable demons attacking him, but it looked like they couldn't get a good hold. I even recognized some of them: envy, gossip, greed. They hovered around him, then slid off like he was a slick surface.

He stepped away from the fountain and saw that I was staring at him. He wiped his mouth self-consciously as he walked toward me. I looked away, and pointed toward my car, forgetting that he had seen me arrive. "It's just over there." When I glanced up at him again, I couldn't see the demons any more.

We didn't talk much in the car. At a traffic light, several gray and white pigeons flew close to the windshield, almost touched down, then thought better of it, their wings filling our view as we leaned forward to watch them sail over the car. I said, "Why can't I see angels? Why does it have to be demons?"

Shay said, "Why would you want to?"

"Who wouldn't want that? They're beautiful, kind, protective." My forehead wrinkled again. I realized I didn't really know what they looked like. When I was attacked, I had seen shimmers of light, followed by the stereotypical "winged man." Was that real, or my brain's idea of what an angel would look like? At the time, he didn't seem anything but powerful and very real.

He laughed. "Angels are usually messengers, not your buddies. They may bring you a task or mission, so be careful what you wish for."

Shay lived a few blocks from the River of Hope Church, in an upscale but comfortable neighborhood. At his driveway, I pulled my car in next to a faded blue sedan. Stickers on the back windshield and bumper proclaimed *"Fear Not"* and *"Surfer."*

"Okay, wait a minute," I said as I cut the engine. "I still need to pay you for that bag." I reached into the back seat for my purse, but he opened his door anyway.

"I'll be right back. I want to get something too. You want a soda?"

"Uh, no, I can't stay long."

"It's right here." I expected him to go inside, but he just popped the trunk of the blue car. I had the check already written out, so I could have just handed it to him I guess, but since he was getting sodas . . . I got out and joined him at his car. Somewhere nearby, a construction vehicle beeped as it backed up in the otherwise quiet street.

He held up two cans. "They're still cold enough. Orange Crush or Coke?" I thanked him and traded him the check for the orange drink. He stuck it in his pocket without looking at it.

"Thanks, El."

"You're welcome."

We leaned against his bumper. The open trunk revealed a box marked *"emergency kits for homeless."* It contained socks, snack food, and toothbrushes. Other boxes were marked *"Bibles"* and *"water bottles."*

"I've spent the last year saving up for art school to study photography, and now I can't go. What's your story?"

"I started at U of H, but had an . . . incident. My parents always had an agreement with me: I could work at a part-time job and get money, or they would give me the same money if I did volunteer work. I did that all through high school, and now I'm taking a year off college to do it again. One reason I started 'The Team,' as we call ourselves, was to give the guys more opportunity to do volunteer work that their parents can't join them for."

"You're like a big brother to them, aren't you?" I purposely ignored the "incident" part. This wasn't a news interview.

He smiled down at his drink, then took a gulp. "I like to think of it that way." He returned my gaze. "Are you still doing the visualization exercise I showed you at the church?"

I took a breath. "That's the other reason I wanted to see you today. I wanted to say thanks for the help, the pointers, but I don't need to keep having lessons with you because I'm going to try another type of therapy to make it stop."

Shay watched me sip my drink. "Are you sure that it should stop? I mean, I know it has been scary for you, especially since you're not used to the idea of the spirit world invading the"—he did air quotes—"'real world.' But it could be useful in some way."

I scowled at the idea of holding on to something so loathsome. "That's what Jon said."

Shay still looked pleasant as he asked, "Jon?"

A spotlight seemed to shine on me. "Oh . . . Jon . . ." My mouth dried and continued to work, like a fish out of water, but no words came out.

Shay laughed. "Are you okay? Who's Jon, your boyfriend?" He glanced away as he said it.

My face burned. I couldn't even begin to think of a lie that would cover the awkward silence. After clearing my throat, I managed to get out, "Jon Addison."

Shay's face didn't fall or become suspicious or guarded. It was more like an earthquake of twenty different emotions passed across it. But he smoothed it out and went on, "The demon guy?"

"That's him; I mean, the guy from the flyer at your church. I saw him at his bookstore event and asked him some questions. I just wanted another opinion . . ." The words that were absent before now flowed out of my mouth in a torrent. *Stop talking, stop talking.* ". . . from, you know, someone who has researched and studied . . . supernatural beings."

Shay's eyes narrowed. "Demons."

Thinking back on our conversations, Jon had often been vague or changed the subject when talking about the details of his business or exactly what these beings were. "He said he can help me."

"Did he tell you anything about his 'research techniques'?" His voice was hard despite the light tone Shay was trying to affect.

"No." I stared at him. *Why can I see demons when it's thoughts I need to see?* "Well yes, hypnotism, I guess." I was embarrassed to admit I really didn't know what to expect from Jon. "Tell me," was all I could say, breathless.

Shay looked in the direction of the beeping sound. I realized it had been beeping continuously. He looked back to me again, a desperate look in his eyes. "Rose saw demons too."

That was the girlfriend that Jon told me about.

"He mentioned her." Why did I feel jealous? Of course Shay had a girlfriend, or many. I would be surprised if he didn't have one. But I had been so distracted by the "girlfriend" part that I hadn't asked Jon for details about what she saw.

"Rose had nightmares about demons at first. No big deal, but then she started seeing them while she was awake. Her parents took her to therapy, then finally had to take her to a psychiatric hospital." He looked me in the eye. "That's where she met Jon."

"He said he was a medical tech there."

"Yeah, but apparently medical science doesn't interest him as much as the idea of demonic possession. Rose's parents were completely taken in by him. The doctor he works with must trust him too."

"But you don't?"

"I don't have any proof." He looked distressed. "But I think Jon is making her worse somehow, for his own research. He's got who knows how much information about The Team from her . . . or from them . . . the demons. He confronted me the last time I went to visit Rose. He said, 'I would give anything to be able to see the future. And I wouldn't screw it up either.' After that, only Rose's parents were allowed to visit her. No friends; definitely not me."

"What are you saying? Jon wants to be a prophet?"

"Or just see the future. He's not interested in the service part of it." He took a last drink and crushed his Coke can. "It's not really a gift most people would want. That's the other reason I started 'The Team;' so I could protect them from people like Jon."

"Do they see demons?"

Shay looked me in the eyes a long moment, then said, "No. But some of them are gifted. They wanted me to form a group so they can work out what they can and can't do. A safe place where they are believed."

"And where they do push-ups."

He laughed at that. "Hey, they choose what we do in 'The Team,' I'm just their coach."

I chewed on that while I sipped my drink. "Do you have a picture of Rose? I want to see her."

Talking to her was what I really wanted, to ask what she saw and whether the demons reacted to her when she looked at them. Getting bits and pieces of information from Jon and Shay was frustrating. I wanted to see her in person, but would settle for a photo. The photo he chose would say as much about him as about her.

Without looking at me, he slowly pulled out his phone, swiped the front, and handed it over. I was dying to look through a whole photo album. But there was Rose, right on the wallpaper. It must be her, because not only did the photo-Shay standing next to her look about one year younger than now, but she was also wearing a necklace with an angel charm—like the one in Jon's kit, but unbroken. His photo showed her softness and vulnerability. Goodness and innocence. And of course, she was beautiful.

I felt sick and angry. I don't know what I had wanted, but something less than in that photo. I wanted to be prettier, smarter, or at least less crazy than her. I didn't know if I could win on any of those.

I saw the time as I handed the phone back. Mariah and I had agreed we would hang out today and cook dinner together tonight. We had hardly seen each other all week.

"I have to go." I wanted to know more about Jon, but if Shay hated him, then I would still have to filter out what was true and what wasn't. My head couldn't take any more today.

He turned back to the trunk. "Wait, I want you to take this." He pulled a Bible from one of the boxes.

"I have one," I responded automatically. My childhood home had a stack of them—literally, as we were not allowed to put anything else on top of the Bible except another Bible.

"Do you read it?" He took my silence as a "no" and held out the Bible.

I stood still. "Thees and thous put me to sleep."

"Okay . . . modern translation." He switched the Bible for another one. "Thees one doesn't have thous." He smiled at me.

Is that Bible humor?

"But you need to actually read it, just showing the cover to the demons won't help."

I took it with a mumbled, "Thank you."

Even though it was midday, the lights on the outside of the garage flickered and came on. The weather was shifting again and clouds were taking over. The shadows and dim light made the yard peaceful and sleepy. The air was getting colder. I started toward my car.

Shay waved. "I wanted to help you, but I spent most of the time talking about myself."

"That's okay," I said. "Bye."

He shut the trunk and leaned against his car. We waved to each other once more as I drove off.

I couldn't see any point in continuing this . . . whatever it was. If Shay couldn't help Rose, he couldn't help me. But was Jon really doing something bad to Rose? I guess if no one else believed in her demons, then no one would question his stirring them up. And even if he was researching demons rather than some kind of angels, so what? Demons were what I was trying to deal with. Since I wasn't under psychiatric care, I could quit if I didn't like his methods. Getting treatment from Jon would burn bridges with Shay, but did that matter? He was too weird to be a friend, and though he was cute, he was apparently someone else's cute guy.

17

Quiet Night In

"No spaghetti on my walls!" Trying to keep a straight face, Mariah stood with her hands on her hips.

I stuck my chin out. "You're not my mom." The spaghetti in my hand was starting to drip on the counter. We were finally home at the same time. The kitchen had never seemed so tiny as we bustled to out-chef each other in meal prep.

"Right, I'm not your mom, so why do I have to keep cleaning up after you?"

I sighed pointedly. "Okay, so it's probably overcooked now."

She dropped the strainer in the sink, and I tipped the pot into it.

"Zee spaghetti, zee is magnifique!" Mariah opened a jar of sauce with a grunt. "And zee sauce, it eez my family's recipe."

"Ah, zee famous recipe stolen by zee grocery store brand sauce?"

She held the generic sauce jar up by her face and posed. "Oui!"

We dumped everything back in the pot along with some micro-waved meatballs and set the table.

After a few mouthfuls, she began to play with her food. "Tell me, what's going on with holy boy and demon guy?

I burst out laughing, barely containing a bite of garlic bread. "Are they superheroes now?"

She raised her eyebrows. "You tell me."

"It's nothing like that. Not with either of them."

I caught her up on the date with Jon and volunteering at the park before driving Shay home.

She continued to wait. I feigned interest in my food, but it was hard to act nonchalant with someone watching every muscle in my face. As I chewed and stared at a corner of the room, trying to look like I was thinking hard, I realized I didn't know where I stood with either one of the guys. Worse, I didn't know where I wanted to be with either one. Was my unease with Jon just fear of getting close? Or was my gut telling me something my brain couldn't?

"Look, you don't have to tell me, but don't go into a whole fantasy sequence with both of them right here at the table."

I laughed again. "No? But I've got garlic breath and spaghetti in my teeth, what better time?"

I wanted to be with a guy I could laugh and have fun with. But these two guys, I didn't think either one wanted me, as a friend or otherwise, so much as they saw me as a means to an end. Mariah was looking at me expectantly again. My body was still, but inside I was floundering.

"I had fun on the date with Jon. He seems nice, and is easy to relax and be myself with. I'm uncomfortable with Shay, but I keep wanting to see him again." She looked surprised. "Maybe not uncomfortable with him, but off-balance. Like he turns everything upside down."

"Why not see them both? You can tell them you don't want to see just one person. They don't need to know who else you're dating."

"Shay has a girlfriend named Rose. She saw demons and got committed to an institution. Well, a hospital. One that Jon works at. Shay doesn't trust Jon and thinks he is the reason he's not allowed to visit her anymore. I don't see that, but Jon is starting to seem a little pushy. He sent me two texts today about how safe hypnotism is. Best case scenario, one guy may be unavailable and the other may be focused on business."

I was losing my appetite as I spoke, but I coiled more spaghetti on my fork so I could avoid her eyes. "I keep hoping that Jon can help me, but he doesn't think seeing demons is a bad thing—despite a girl getting locked up over them."

Jon had been careful to avoid calling his "wordly angels" words like "demons," but what else were they? Just thinking about it made that panicky feeling start up in the back of my head again, just like when . . .

I looked up. Mariah tore her bread into bits as she listened to me, eating just the garlic butter topping. I focused on the panicky feeling. I blinked, and her demon was back. Or had it never left? "Mariah, I want to try something." I met her eyes, and she raised her eyebrows. "The demons are still disappearing and reappearing, and I'm trying to figure out why."

"Oh?" She sat motionless, eyes not leaving my face.

"Yes." I nodded. "I can see it on you again. If I can figure this out, maybe I can make it stop."

As if in silent agreement, we both pushed our plates to the side.

"You can't control it consciously?" Her brow was wrinkled as if she could squeeze the thoughts out through her face. "But you think there's a logical reason for it?"

"Um, yeah. I don't know why it started in the first place, so why it would stop and start is even more beyond me."

"Sure, but think of it like an illness; while you look for the root cause so you can cure it, see what you can do about the symptoms."

"Okay, let's go with that. What do I do to control my sneezing, coughing, aching, seeing creatures from the depths of hell?"

She scowled at me. "Yeah, like I've never seen one of those at six a.m." She caught herself. "I'm sorry, that was . . ."

"It was funny, don't worry." I patted her arm.

Mariah took a small breath and looked down very hard at her clasped hands on the table. "When I was a kid and had a problem—with my mom or getting moved to my dad's or . . . anything—I learned to focus on it closely, like I had it under a microscope. Instead of running away from a problem"—she looked at me—"not that you're running away . . ."

"I get it." I nodded for her to go on.

"Instead, I would stand still and look at it without blinking. Examine the parts of it and all. The colors, the textures. It would make the problem look smaller, easier to handle."

"Yeah, but Mariah, this is . . ."

She gave me the look she reserved for dead serious situations. "El, I was ten. You're eighteen. The whole world is big and scary when you're ten."

"Agreed. So, what do I focus on?"

"What were you thinking about before you saw it?"

As I tried to think, I stared at the menacing thing absentmindedly. It turned slowly, looking over its shoulder at me. Its upper lip curled back over tiny teeth.

"About Shay . . . and Jon," I said finally.

"In what way? What were you feeling?"

"Curious, maybe frustrated, because I don't know what's going on with them. What they are up to or what they want from me." I felt a prickle of anger, and there was something soothing about its familiarity. I looked at her face again. "I mean really, each of them can seem so great one minute, and the next I feel like they are using me." I frowned. *Jerks. Just be honest with me.*

I felt bad for calling them jerks and looked down, then back at Mariah. The demon was gone.

"Sure," she said, "that would be . . ."

"It worked." I stared at her in disbelief. "Mariah, it's gone."

"What? But how?"

"Let's see . . . I was angry. I was complaining about how the guys go from nice to making me feel caught in their rivalry. I keep trying to figure them out. Shay in particular, how could anyone be so nice and caring? Does he do it from a sense of guilt . . ."

My mouth dropped open. The demon was back. I simply pointed. Mariah tensed her shoulders and dropped them again, looking away. I wanted to tell her that if it's there, it's there all the time, not just when I see it, but I guessed that would not be comforting.

"Uh, so if I think about what's going on with these guys, I see demons, and if I think about myself, they go away? That sounds backward."

"What do you mean?" Mariah still seemed hesitant to consider that there could be any normal side at all to seeing the denizens of hell on her favorite sweater.

"If I'm selfish and moody and blaming other people, then I don't see them, but if I try to understand what makes someone else tick, then I see demons. It's like being punished for doing something good. I need to think this over."

***

The rest of the evening was relaxing and fun. We watched a Christmas movie that had us both laughing, and I used the distraction of it to peek sideways at Mariah while experimenting with the effect of my thoughts on my visions. By the time we had finished the popcorn and the movie credits rolled, I could turn it on and off pretty reliably. I mentally cheered for myself—it seemed like a huge victory. The only hiccup was when it seemed like the hero of the movie had died, and I couldn't turn the sight off until I was sure he was okay. Or until I was okay; it was a sad scene.

Watching the movie kept me up later than usual, and I slept like a rock till early morning.

The dream started like most dreams. Just me, muddling through my day trying to find something that kept changing into something else. Mariah may have said she used to be a mermaid, I can't remember for sure. Then Shay appeared and looked into my eyes before kissing me and stroking my hair back behind my ear.

I began to wake. I was in a shadowy room on a hospital bed. I touched my lips where Shay had kissed me in the dream. A dark figure walked in—I was annoyed at the interruption. Without warning, the figure cut the sheet open over my body, and split open my torso. I gasped and looked up, but couldn't see a face. I knew it was a demon. I felt no pain, just fear. The demon turned into a ball of light and flew into my chest.

I prayed, "Oh God, please save me. Jesus, please save me."

I heard a roaring noise up and to my right—in the corner of the room. The demon was there. I only saw it as patterns of colored light, like a kaleidoscope. Then I heard it speak, but not in any language I had ever heard before. Its voice was angry and rough. I was still praying over and over, "Help me Jesus, please."

It didn't go away all at once. The light and voice left quickly, but I still felt some presence of it inside me. I kept praying. There was nothing else I could do, nothing I could hold on to. An odd, uncomfortable feeling in my chest was the last remainder of the demon's presence. Eventually, it faded to nothing.

Struggling to sit up, the sheets seemed extra long as I fought to free my arms. Fully awake at last and wiping sweat from my face, I looked around the room to reassure myself that I was alone.

Just when I thought things were as bad as they could get, a new level of fear presented itself. Since they had never touched me, I had thought they never would. Of course, it was only a dream. Or so I hoped.

18

Unexpected Visitor

A couple more days of practice had me confident in my ability to turn off the sight most of the time, but I still felt the tension of knowing, or at least believing, there was a demon nearby, even when I wasn't looking at it. Stress of the things normal people worry about was mounting too. Christmas was less than a week away, and I hadn't mailed my Christmas cards.

Yawning, walking in to work, my phone buzzed.

"Hello?"

"Well, hello stranger!"

"Hi, Mom." I could not think of one pleasant thing to add to that.

"I haven't heard from you in so long, I was worried."

"I've been . . . busy. You know, Christmas shopping, working . . ." *Deciding where I stand in the battle of good versus evil, you know—busy.*

"The ladies at the salon asked about my kids, and I was so embarrassed that I couldn't tell them what you've been up to. I had to make something up."

"Tell them my boyfriend dumped me, and I'm working as a photographer." It actually didn't hurt so bad to say it.

"If this is a bad time, I can call you later."

"Uh, okay. I'll talk to you later then. I love you."

"Love you too." And with an air kiss to the phone, she was gone. It was the shortest, easiest conversation we had ever had. *Maybe I should say what I'm thinking more often.*

***

I had been ignoring texts from both of the guys while I tried to figure things out.

John texted: *"El, I know what I'm doing."* And later, *"Now, the question is—do you trust me? Because I can't help you if you don't."*

Shay texted: *"Darkness cannot drive out darkness; only light can do that."*

I spent a lot of time on the studio computer looking up Bible verses before I discovered it was a Martin Luther King, Jr. quote.

***

After a few hours of work, I didn't have any more clients and got off early. I used the extra time to address my Christmas cards. The break room table was sticky, so I moved to the studio reception area. Then Susan kept talking at me and clients kept bumping the table, so I shoved everything back in my tote bag and moved to the mall food court. The fountain provided some white noise to drown out the surrounding conversations.

As I was sticking on the last stamp, the movement of the fountain caught my eye. I watched the shimmers of light reflected by the water onto the ceiling. I thought of the shimmery light of the angel I had seen during the attempted abduction. I wanted to see another one. Was there a way to contact them? I thought of Jon's "worldly angel" kit and shivered. It was supposed to teach you to attract your "helper," but I didn't think that was the kind of spiritual being I was looking for. Last time I was in trouble, an angel intervened. I saw the answer and rejected it at the same time: danger. I thought of those cold eyes as the man dragged me to his SUV. I didn't want to see an angel that badly. But what if I were in just a little danger, something I could control?

My mind whirling, I headed for the car. To turn on the sight, I focused on my never-ending circle of thoughts about Shay—did he still love Rose, why did he do what he did . . . I checked the couple walking toward me in the parking lot and saw reptilian shapes pressed against their throats, confirming that my sight was switched on.

Otherwise, I didn't put much thought into what I was doing as I made my way to Memorial Drive. Since it was set up like a highway with feeder roads, I could get my speed up without endangering cyclists or dogs. I entered a twisty section of the road, way over the speed limit. My adrenaline charged up as the car hugged first one curve, then another. I kept looking, but no visible angels. Now what? Did I have to be in the process of crashing? My stomach tightened uncomfortably. I reconsidered the whole thing, but I couldn't think of another way.

I was almost at the end of the curvy part of the road; it was now or never. I bit my lip and pushed the accelerator further. And then I saw lights—but they were blue flashing lights.

The police officer took his time getting to my window. I tried not to think bitter thoughts about where he had been the night I was in trouble. The officer's lips were pressed into a thin line as he took my paperwork. As he wrote the ticket, I imagined kissing my new Christmas money goodbye and letting it flutter away in the wind.

I drove toward home five miles per hour below the limit to be safe from further tickets and to thumb my nose at the whole world. If I was annoyed, everyone else could be too. And they were; they showed it by tailgating, then cutting around me abruptly.

I was only a block from home when I slowed further for a good reason. I keep a sharp eye out for children, toys, and animals, because they all end up in the street. Just ahead, a boy and a girl were running down the sidewalk next to a park. The girl, who was bigger, was gaining on the boy. To escape, he cut suddenly to the side and went into the street. I was ready and stopped without jamming the brake. I decided not to blow the horn and scare the kid.

I should have, though.

A green hatchback cut around me on my left. The girl had stopped near the curb, wide-eyed. But the boy's momentum carried him to the middle of my lane, right in the path of the car cutting in front of me.

Time seemed to slow down. I blew the horn and yelled, "Look out!" *Please God, don't let it happen.* And in that slo-mo sliver of time, I saw a shimmer of light push the girl into the street and pull her all the way back to the curb, the boy in her arms.

The hatchback slowed, already in the spot where the boy had stood, then sped off faster than ever. I looked at the kids—the girl looked as amazed as she did relieved. The boy looked like he was gearing up for a massive crying fit once he got over the shock. The shimmery shape stroked the boy's hair, his cheek, and then was gone. The girl looked at me resentfully and pulled the boy back toward the park. Just like that, everything was back to normal. I drove home.

The apartment complex pool area was quiet, the chairs dusty from lack of use. Winter was so short in Houston, you could almost swim year-round, but they didn't clean the pool in the winter. Bits of leaves made swirly shapes on the bottom as the late afternoon sunlight angled down half-heartedly. The water cast weblike reflections that rose and fell on the fence. Even though it was chilly out, I sat in one of the mesh chairs, my keys still in my hand, along with

Shay's Bible. I had carried it to the poolside to flip through it for any information on angels. Then I thought of visions; didn't Daniel have visions? I found the book of Daniel.

"I, Daniel, was the only one who saw the vision; those who were with me did not see it, but such terror overwhelmed them that they fled and hid themselves. So I was left alone, gazing at this great vision . . ." I knew what it was like to feel alone.

It certainly wasn't worth endangering anyone to try to see angels again, and I couldn't talk to them if they were going to appear and disappear so quickly. But what would I say even if I could? I leaned forward over the edge of the pool, stretching my hand out to catch the reflected light on my skin. A shadow fell on the water and blocked the light of the sun.

"Don't fall in; it's too cold to jump in after you."

Jon's voice was as mellow and musical as ever, but he sounded a bit off somehow. I looked up at him, but could only see his silhouette against the glare.

"I guess you could kick the chair in after me—they float." I smiled in his direction, squinting, but still couldn't see his features. He turned his head as if looking around and moved closer.

"I left you a message to say I was in the neighborhood, but when I didn't hear back, I thought I would just drop by."

"I didn't hear my phone . . ."

"I've found a way to end your visions, and I thought you might be interested."

I couldn't breathe for a moment. Could it be true?

I waited so long to answer that I could feel an awkwardness creeping in. Was I making him uncomfortable by sitting there, being unresponsive? Or was he embarrassed at reaching out and being ignored? I knew that feeling too, and would never wish it on anyone else. But his worldly angels held little interest for me now that I was pursuing the other kind.

Jon hunkered down beside my chair. "I was talking with Rose earlier, and my associate and I had a new idea. If you want to come to my office, we can try it." I could finally see his face. He looked older somehow, tired and yet intense. The mention of Rose got my attention. He worked with Rose. Would I be able to see her if I went to his office? I was burning with curiosity. I wondered whether she was truly insane, or if she was like me. Assuming I wasn't insane, of course. But maybe my recent discoveries could help her.

He pulled the Bible out of my hands and peered at it as he stood up again. "I can tell you what you need to know, no reading required." I stared at the book. Did he really just take the Bible away from me? He flipped through it and leaned back against the fence.

I still hated using the sight, but I wanted to be safe. I turned it on as I looked at him. The sun shone on half his face, which was calm. He spread his arms and leaned his elbows on the pool fence behind him for balance . . . or for showing off his chest, which was worth showing off. No demons. I was a little surprised he didn't have even one, but okay. I turned the sight off again.

"Yeah, I'll go with you."

19

The Kiss

Something nagged at the back of my mind as I followed Jon to his car and got in. But I should be happy: if Jon's hunch was right, this might be my last day to see demons. As much as I wanted that, I found myself more intrigued by Rose.

Keeping my voice casual, I asked, "Will I get to meet Rose today?"

He laughed and kept his eyes on the road as he drove. "Rose is a bit of a recluse. Probably for the best; she has to wear a locator device that beeps when she wanders off. She has an almost supernatural ability to escape." He smiled at some private joke.

Odd that she would be under such heavy security—it had seemed like she had a problem similar to mine, but not anything violent or directly harmful. And surely she was on her way to some kind of cure.

I waited for him to say more and got annoyed when he didn't. I sighed and looked around. The car was mostly tidy. It had a layer of dust on the hood that it didn't have when I saw it at the bookstore. The check engine light was on, and there was an orange sticky note on the control panel that read *"focus."*

"You talked to her today, right? So maybe she's still in a talkative mood. It might be nice to compare notes."

He slowed at a stoplight, looking around like he was considering running it. "Rose is at the hospital. I said we're going to my office."

"I guess I thought your office was at the hospital—where you work."

"That's one job. My private business has to be handled outside the hospital. Too many rules there."

I realized I was in a car with a man I barely knew, going God knows where, and we might be the only ones in his office. The itchy thought at the back of my head finally surfaced. *How did he know where I live?* I tried to reason with myself. It was a big city; as long as his office wasn't in his home, there should be people around. *I hope.*

"Are you hungry?" I asked. "Maybe we could just discuss this at dinner instead of at your office. I'm hungry."

He considered a moment. "There are some good places near the office, but we should take care of business first or the office staff will be gone."

"Oh, okay. If we're not talking to Rose, what are we doing? What is it that you found out that can help me?"

He was concentrating on making a left turn, waiting for space in the oncoming line of cars. "They said that hypnotism is the only way."

"I don't want to—Jon, I already told you I don't want to be hypnotized. Who said it's the only way?"

He stepped on the gas and made the turn on a yellow light. He glanced toward me with a miffed look, then concentrated on the road again. "Won't it be wonderful to look at people normally again? Sleep through the whole night without nightmares?" His right eye started to twitch.

Another quick left took us into the parking lot of a plain three-story brick building. He turned off the engine and said, "Let's go."

Why didn't I drive my own car here? I needed to start thinking quicker. I couldn't order a ride service with a non-smart phone, but it didn't seem like it was worth making a scene about. He would simply have to think of a treatment other than hypnotism. I stuck the Bible on the seat and got out to follow.

It was just an ordinary office building. Downright boring, in fact. The lobby was silent with tall, green potted palms. Going up the lobby stairs to the second floor, I could hear a cleaning crew starting their shift. We passed doors labeled for sports medicine, counseling, and a nonprofit for children with cancer. The final door's nameplate had a list of names, including *"Jon Addison, LLC."*

Inside, half a dozen offices circled a central reception area. Most had their doors shut and lights off. A pudgy sofa and chairs gave the anteroom a cozy feel. Beyond them, a receptionist's desk and small business center lay in front of the one office still lit.

The woman at the desk had a phone cradled between her neck and shoulder. She waved excitedly at Jon when she saw him. She spoke into the phone with a thick Texas drawl. "Oh, sir – sir, could you hold for just one second?" She poked the hold button and held the phone gleefully toward Jon. "Mr. Addison, that man you were waiting to hear from, at the production company, just called. I've got him on hold now."

"Kelly, please try to sound more professional when you get calls for me."

Her face fell, and she clutched the phone to her breast. "What? What did I say?" Every word was drawn out like it was in slow motion.

Jon sighed and gestured for her to hand over the receiver. "Just give it to me." Kelly, looking befuddled, handed it to him. He waved me into his office as she pushed the hold button again. I shared an apologetic glance as I walked past her.

Jon's office was classic and clinical and polished. You could make calls, hold meetings, or interview patients here. It was so tidy, though, that I wondered if he did any of that. I sat in one of the chairs in front of his desk and immediately popped up again, uncomfortable being a "patient." Or even a client.

Out in the reception area, Jon laughed boisterously. It sounded fake. The chance of a job will do that to you. Or trying to achieve a dream. *Why am I so suspicious of him?* I peeked out the door to be sure Kelly wasn't going to come in to check on me. She was doodling sullenly on a notepad. I went back to the desk.

Business must be good. His desk was gorgeous, some exotic wood, definitely not the type you would expect for the average hospital employee. The surface was bare except for a matching pencil cup and inbox. Three papers sat in the inbox, and two freshly sharpened pencils rested in the cup. Were they for show? Who uses regular pencils anymore? Something like a postcard leaned against the pencil cup. A thick, expensive-looking pen lay parallel to his smart phone. Didn't he say he called me while in the neighborhood? I leaned closer. Oddly, the reminder on the phone was telling him to eat dinner.

Moving to the side of the desk revealed the card was actually a photo of Rose. Not in a frame, just propped up against the pencil cup. I studied the photo as a photographer. Reality and fantasy are in delicate balance in photography. People pay large amounts of money to have photos look a certain way, not to show what their humdrum life really looks like. This looked like a rejected proof to me, because Rose looked hard and closed off. Since this was the photo sitting on his desk, it's likely that this was how Jon wanted to see her.

He was still on the receptionist's phone, his hearty laugh echoing in the quiet office. What info could I find on his "treatment" for Rose here? I rounded the desk and slid open the center drawer. Normal office stuff: paper clips, correction tape, some coins, Post-its, all contained in little boxes. The file drawer contained dark blue hanging folders with their plastic tabs all lined up like soldiers. Names of men and women were printed on them, last names first, but not in alphabetical order. I peeked in the first one and saw a score sheet with *"#2"* written in the top right corner. The fourth folder had a *"#5"* at the top. I slid the drawer shut and listened. Jon sounded like he was confirming information as he wrote it down.

The top right drawer had more dull stuff—still all neat and sparse and utilitarian and unused looking. Watching the doorway, I closed the right and pulled open the top left-hand drawer at the same time to hide the noise of multiple drawers. If Jon walked in I could say I was looking for gum.

I looked down . . . into the mouth of hell. Well, okay, not really. But it was as close as I wanted to ever be. An electric razor, clogged with what had to be several days' growth of beard. Bloody tissue. Eye cream, caffeine pills, 5-hour Energy. Big, untidy clusters of sticky notes with single words scrawled on them like *"devour,"* *"mine,"* *"carcass,"* and *"now."* There were also several items that looked like they had been broken apart in a rage—pens, earbud wires, and a wooden ruler splintered from its bent metal edge. Three prescription bottles were clustered in the corner.

Reaching for one of the pill bottles, I jumped when I heard the phone clack down onto its cradle. I tried to slide the drawer closed with both hands to keep it quiet, but the razor's cord had risen up and the drawer stuck. I pushed it down, but that pushed the razor and the caffeine pills up, and it stuck again. I started to panic, poking things down as I pushed harder on the drawer.

"Idiot!" The shout made me jump again, accidentally jerking the drawer farther out. "Do you still not understand what I am trying to do here?" I realized Jon was shouting at Kelly. I shook the drawer a little, the noise no longer an issue, and the contents settled enough that I could shut it.

Kelly spluttered something and Jon raged on, "You are the front door for what could be a national business. I want to be known across the country, not just in one corner of one city, but I can't do that if the woman answering the phone sounds like a hick on her way to a country dance!"

It seemed foolish to risk being caught snooping while he was so angry, but I was less thrilled than ever at the idea of Jon's hypnotizing me and getting inside my head. If this was going to be my only visit to his office, it had to count. Only one more drawer. I looked up at the door. It was quieter out there, but I could still hear his voice.

I slid open the last drawer just enough to be sure I could close it again. It contained two folders. I opened it farther. A fat blue folder, ragged at the edges, had the name *"Riley, Rose"* on the tab. Some of the papers poked out and I could see *"#1"* written in the top corner of a page. A thin beige manila folder below it had *"Williams, Eliana"* handwritten on the tab. The front sheet had *"#1.5"* written in the upper corner. A crumpled paper on top of it had a messy scrawl that read *"I helped you—you owe—give us the girl—I owe them—everything has a price."*

"Eliana?" Jon stood at the door.

I froze like a hunted rabbit. He couldn't see the open drawer from where he was, but I didn't dare shut it yet in case there was any chance he might still go back out.

"I'm sorry you had to hear that." His eyes dropped to the desk. "My phone." He looked like a kid at Christmas and started toward me. I grabbed the phone and stretched forward to hand it to him, shoving the drawer shut with my leg. There was a loud *whump,* and I faked surprise.

"Ow, my knee." I held the phone out to him with one hand and rubbed my knee with the other. He rushed over to look, but I waved him off. "It's okay, I just bumped it."

He took the phone out of my hand and glanced at the reminder on the screen, then his eyes cut back to me. "What were you doing?"

"Looking at Rose's photo." That could explain my guilty look as well as anything.

Looking down at the desk and where I stood, he opened his mouth to speak, but Kelly appeared at the door. I took the opportunity to walk back to where I had left my purse in front of his desk.

"Mr. Addison." Kelly seemed to be trying to speak without an accent, but it just made her talk slower. "I wouldn't bother you, but Doug isn't here, and I need someone to sign my time sheet." She looked a bit sick.

"Miss Jones, accounting will not hold your check back just because I did not sign your paperwork at seven o'clock at night." I glanced at the clock out in reception; it was six o'clock.

She tried another way, walking forward and holding out the paper and a pen. "It'll just take you a second."

It seemed like he would yank it out of her hand, but he took it calmly and placed it on his desk to sign it with a flourish. He held it out to her without a word. She looked away from his gaze, and looked me in the face. I could see tears in her eyes. Kelly seemed lonely, sad. Stuck. I saw a demon appear on her collarbone. It looked as happy as she looked sad. Its toothy mouth opened in a grin that got wider and wider still. Was it turning inside out? Something dark began flowing out of its mouth like a black cloud. It shuddered, and the last of the cloud was out. The darkness floated to the woman's chest and sank into her. Tears flowed down her cheeks now. She took the time sheet from Jon and said, "Thank you, Mr. Addison. I'm so sorry I upset you. I've just been having problems at home, and here at work, and it's just all coming apart."

I was still gaping at her chest. What was that cloud that went inside her?

Jon picked up on the way I was looking at Kelly as she scurried out. I tensed even before I met his eyes and saw the gleam in them.

"What is it? Did you see something? On Kelly?"

Tears threatened to come up; I was panicking and trying to fight it. "I, uh . . ."

"It's okay." He was about as soothing as a snake. "Have a seat. Can I get you something? Are you thirsty?"

This was the start of it. He was going to get me settled in—alone with him—and do his voodoo on me. And I didn't mean sex. It had been stupid to think he would bring me here to help me. I had to get out.

"I thought we were going to go eat," I said weakly, scratching at my moist right eye.

"What if we try something to take care of your demon problem first? I'm curious to see just how powerful your sight is." He leaned with one hand on his desk, but his eye was twitching again. "If I can get you to open up and let me speak to whatever is causing this, you'll feel so much better."

One side of my mind calculated the odds of success with different strategies while the other side tried to keep up the light conversation. What would work best? Crying? Demanding he take me home? A word floated up to my conscious mind: negotiate. That sounded doable. The answer popped into my head.

"Christmas Eve."

"What?"

I pushed myself like never before. I smiled like a model and tilted my head. "Jon," I said, "wouldn't you rather hypnotize me on camera?"

The conflict was easy to read in his eyes, his face, the twitch in his right hand.

"Christmas Eve is your big day." I tried to bat my eyelashes, but wasn't sure how fast to blink.

He considered another moment. "You'll do that?" I had him.

"Yeah, I'll get my fifteen minutes of fame too." I didn't have to fake the laugh that followed; I was so relieved he was going along with it.

He pulled out his keys and jingled them. "Let's go eat. I'm hungry too." He walked by Kelly's desk without looking at her. I followed him out.

The short car ride to the restaurant was quiet, because he kept checking texts he had missed on his phone earlier. I considered trying to get out of dinner also, but guessed I was temporarily out of danger since he wanted the on-camera hypnotism so badly. Better to keep him calm for a while. I pointed out a deli, because I figured we could get in and out quickly. We sat at a red and white formica table to wait for our orders.

"So how did you first meet Rose?"

"Ah, but your friend Shay told you that already, didn't he?"

"He said that you do some kind of research with Rose . . . on her demons."

"And that I pay her hospital bills. He told you that?"

"No." That was a surprise.

A server arrived with our food. He ignored her and went on, "I pay Rose's bills with money from my business, which functions with information I get from Rose. See how that all works?"

"Yes." I let the word sit there.

He started to eat. I moved my food around, looking for my appetite. When the silence became uncomfortable, he said, "She is in a mental hospital. They are trying to understand her illness. To give her therapy. I just do my research in between what the doctors are doing anyway. Her parents are aware."

"What do you do?"

I never thought he would come clean, but he did. "I stimulate the demonic attacks. I bring them to the forefront so I can talk to them and watch their reactions. I have been trying for months to get new information from them. It's not enough anymore to just get material things; I want to know the future."

Rather than feeling relieved at his honesty, I was terrified. He was either insane or cold-blooded. And since he was employed at a mental hospital, I guessed it was the latter.

"Like info on what the stock market will do? How would demons know about that or anything in the future?"

He smiled. "There is the material world"—he waved his hands around—"and there is the spiritual world." His fingers flew out like a magician making a scarf disappear. "The spiritual world is not bound by the concept of time, since those beings are outside of time."

I tried to wrap my mind around that. He continued, "All times are now, this moment, all at once." Nope, not wrapping; I'd just have to take his word on that one.

"And 'now' the stock market is up ten years from now?"

"Part of it is, part of it isn't." He took a big swig of his iced tea. "You're still thinking small, Ellie. What products will be the new microchip, the iPhone? Who will invent them? Who will be the president?"

My face probably paled a bit at being called "Ellie."

He leaned forward, bread crumbs on the side of his mouth. "On Christmas Eve, I have a very special therapy session planned. Rose's parents will take her out for a visit to my office—there's less chance of interference there. I'll have you on camera first for a demonstration of reaching greater psychic vibrations with hypnotism. Then I will push Rose further than I ever have. It will force them to tell me what I want."

I felt cold at the mention of my part in this. But my curiosity kept me from arguing about it. "You can force them to do things? A human can do that?"

"If you know what you're doing." He chuckled. "They have to answer, or destroy their host. Too much thrashing around, resisting —even though it's not physical movement, it does a lot of damage. So I get my business information, and we learn more about the condition, which helps other patients."

"The condition?"

"Demonic inhabitation." He laughed, then sobered again quickly as he looked more closely at me. "That's . . . not what we'll do with you, of course. Not at all."

It wasn't comforting, or believable. To break eye contact, I started shoving food in my mouth.

"What does that do to Rose?"

I think my horrified look finally got through to him. His demeanor changed to serious, even concerned. "Rose was already very unwell. I'm only thinking of the future . . . of medical science. I can be open with you about these things because I want you to be a business partner, but we'll talk more at the taping." Jon finished his wrap and onion rings and licked his fingers.

Taking a breath, I opened up, turned on my vision, and looked up at him. Nothing happened. I tried harder. *Come on, concentrate. Open up, look.* He had to have some kind of demon.

"Eliana? Are you okay?" I was looking so hard, I forgot he was right in front of me, looking back at me.

"Sure, I'm fine." I laughed. "Um, just thought about all I need to do—shopping, decorating. Christmas Eve is coming." I fussed with my napkin and finished off my drink.

Jon had no demons on him. How was that possible? I shot a glance around the restaurant. Everyone else had something nagging at them. Shay practically had a cloud of them diving at him. Was it because of Jon's work? Maybe he really knew how to control them? But he didn't help Kelly with whatever she had on her. And I didn't have any demons either, for reasons unknown; I figured they avoided me because I could see them.

"Shall we?" Jon was jovial again. We both stood.

I picked up my purse, and my hand touched the business card from Shay with his phone and address. Somehow, it had risen to the top of the jumbled items in my purse. I pushed it back in, and another idea occurred to me. "If you know her problem is demons, you could just set her free, couldn't you? I mean, drive out the demons?"

Just as he turned away to put his drink down on the table, I looked over at him. My heart stopped.

Flat against his back was an enormous demon. It was many shades of green. Forest to olive to gray-green, as if layers of its skin had grown over time. Like tree bark or sedimentary rock. Its wide, flat form had allowed it to conform to Jon's back, hidden from me despite its size. The only part that stuck out were the knobby shapes around its head, like a crown was sprouting from its skull. It saw me looking at it and snarled at me.

Jon whirled to face me.

"You certainly make snap decisions about things you never knew until five minutes ago." My eyes were wide after seeing the demon, but they opened farther at this rebuke. Jon softened. "Sorry—must be more tired than I realized. I don't know where that came from."

He rubbed his eyes and steadied himself. "But how many others will suffer the same fate if we don't learn all we can from her?"

He smiled and put his hand on my back as we walked to the door. I held my breath and looked at anything but him as we left the restaurant. *Oh God, please don't let that thing near me!*

On the walk to the car, the sight wouldn't turn off, maybe because I was so freaked out. Just knowing that thing was on him made my stomach churn. How much of it was in what Jon did or said? How much was it controlling him?

"I'm sorry, let me get that for you."

I realized I was standing still, staring at the passenger door of his car. Jon rushed to open it for me. I felt my face get warm. I didn't smile or say thank you for his opening the door. He shut it gently as I settled in, and walked around to the driver's side.

Jon was dangerous and knew where I lived. I had something he wanted, and that thing was part of me. How could I get away from him permanently? What had I done to make my ex-jerk Chas leave? I could be nice, devoted, and promise to build my life around him. That should have him pushing me out of the car as we drove past my building. Jon was rattling away about something. I pulled myself together and listened, but still avoided looking at him.

". . . will be a big deal, and I mean deal in the literal sense too. This is my shot at the big time—national talk shows, book deal, maybe my own TV show."

Why can't people start a sentence with "maybe my own TV show?" Then maybe I would listen to all of what they're saying instead of wishing I had heard how we got there. I couldn't see his demon anymore; focusing on myself must have allowed the sight to turn off. I was curious to see if it was interacting with him, but I hated seeing demons, and his was scarier than most, so I just studied Jon's face instead.

"You have a perspective no one else has." His voice took on an awestruck sound. "I mean, no one in the Bible ever saw anything like you do. You are the first to be able to tell humankind what is . . . out there."

Daniel's name was on the tip of my tongue, but something nudged my gut. It wasn't just a vague feeling; I put my hand on my belly and could almost feel the tense knot there. *Wait.* The word bubbled up in my mind.

"Eliana? Are you okay? It's all pretty exciting. There's so much potential." We were parked at the apartment building, and Jon smiled at me. I smiled back.

"It is exciting. I'm very happy for you." The words flowed. I would find a way to end this and hear about what happens from a distance. Whatever it was he was doing. I wish I had listened.

"For me? You mean for us. When Rose's demons spill their guts to me and their prophecies come true—well, my predictions as far as the world will know—I'll be the most sought-after man on Earth. A prophet of biblical proportions." He looked at me as if he thought I already knew this. "And like I said, you'll be there with me, helping me find more subjects."

"Huh? What do you mean more subjects?"

Again he seemed to find this amusing. "Rose can't survive the habitation much longer, and it's only the deeply rooted demons, the ones that get to the heart, that are of use to me. Since you can see them, you can help me find a new 'Rose' faster than I can on my own. And I really can't be a prophet if my source dries up and I don't have a replacement. I'm sure you wouldn't want to take her place."

Was that a threat? It was like he was handing me calculus problems during a movie. Even without knowing her, Rose didn't deserve this. She wasn't disposable. And I wasn't going to find replacements for her. My forehead was starting to hurt from being so creased with concentration. "And why would I help you?"

He laughed charmingly, like we were flirting with each other. "You'll be well paid, of course. You'll be able to keep your youth indefinitely. On a more practical level, you can't tell on me, or you would sound crazy. If I merely said I was talking to demons, I would sound crazy. But I'm not going to say that. I'll say I had visions of the future—which, yes, will sound crazy at first, but then they'll come true."

He shut off the engine, and cold air seeped in. He turned toward me and lowered his voice. "And you will help me. You haven't seen how they live, in the institution. They're treated well enough I guess . . . for insane people. But their every movement has to be monitored, approved, controlled . . . for their own good, of course. It's like you don't own your body anymore. You don't want to be one of them. You've already left a trail of people who know you've been hallucinating. It wouldn't be hard to come up with enough evidence."

The threat cut me deep. A real, bone-deep terror started to take hold of me as he continued to hold my gaze. His face filled my vision, and everything else blurred. Then he leaned a bit closer, and his eyes softened. Just knowing what was coming and my brain going into high alert caused my sight to slip into action again. One of the gray-green demon's bloodshot eyes came into view as its face slid up behind Jon's head, looking down at me.

"Give us a kiss," Jon whispered. He closed his eyes and pressed his lips to mine.

20

Epiphany

I got out fast, wiping the moisture off my lips. After slamming the car door, I ran to the apartment, shoved open the door, and ran to the kitchen sink. Retching, I rinsed my mouth and spat before splashing my whole face, as if it would wash away the memory. The dish towel scrunched against my face felt warm and comforting. My throat ached from gagging, and tears filled my eyes.

He must know. He researches demons; how could he not realize one was holding on to him? A sick feeling enveloped me.

Did I know—or not know—what may be holding on to me?

I knew it was useless to look in the mirror, but went to the bathroom anyway, shedding shirt, pants, and socks on the way. Mariah wouldn't be home for hours. I could see demons on others with their clothes on, but I felt dirty somehow, like I needed to strip away all I could.

There was nothing in the mirror, of course. I ran my hands down my bare legs as I looked, as if checking for ticks. Nothing. Twisted each leg to look at the back. Nothing. Nothing. My arms, my—wait, what if it was on my head? I ran my fingers through my hair, but I wouldn't be able to see it or feel it, nor would anyone else. I twisted, trying to see my lower back—which was hard—and could see my hips were clear.

Close to giving up, I lifted and twisted my left shoulder, craning my neck to look down my back. And screamed.

A pair of eyes stared back at me. The gray-green face pinched inward as it crouched closer to my shoulder and snarled at me. It had a bumpy head that made it look like a small, ugly queen with a lumpy crown. Gasping, I turned forward again.

This can't be happening. I thought I was special, gifted. I thought I was the seer, not the victim. It can't be real, I'm ...

I pushed my shoulder as far forward as it would go and carefully twisted my neck back again. Its lips were moving in time with the words in my head: *special, gifted ...*

Pain shot through my neck from twisting it so far.

Panicking, I swatted blindly at my shoulder with first one hand, then the other. I could reach better from above with my right hand, but I couldn't see it and reach it at the same time. I would look unhinged to anyone watching me. And maybe I was. I already knew I couldn't touch them with my hands, but I struggled anyway. And it stayed attached.

But I'm not like the others ... I'm special, gifted ...

I ran to the living room and grabbed the Bible where I'd dropped it. I flipped through it manically, tearing a page in my haste. I had no idea where to find how to get rid of demons and wasn't about to look through the index, so I started reading anything my eye fell on out loud.

"Will the one who contends with the Almighty correct him?" I flipped back toward the front. "God gave Solomon wisdom and very great insight ..." I clawed at my shoulder again. I could barely look to the left due to the painful crick in my neck. But out of the corner of my eye, I saw the silent snarling creature staring me down again. I flipped toward the end. "There is no one righteous, not even one; there is no one who understands . . ." Crying, scared, hopeless, and now in pain every time my neck moved, I swatted at my back with the Bible as I sank to the floor.

It's part of you, a dark voice inside me said. *You are prideful. You cannot help it, but why should you?*

"No, no, no," I moaned into the carpet, stripped to my underwear and huddled like a whimpering dog. Pitiful.

You were chosen above the others, to see what they cannot.

The words sounded flattering, so why did they have a nasty edge to them?

21

Shay's House

Shay's card stayed in my front jeans pocket on the frantic drive to his house. It felt protective somehow. I couldn't remember exactly where his house was, but when I thought I was close, I spotted his car parked at a white frame house with a big, decorative cross by the door. I pulled my car into the driveway and slammed the brakes. "Shay!" There was no way he could hear me yet, but I screamed it anyway. A curtain moved at a downstairs window. I ran out of the car, not sure if I had shut the door, but not looking back.

He flung the door open and met me on the porch. "Eliana?" I was grateful for the concern on his face.

"I have a demon! Oh Shay, there's one on me." I guess I emphasized the last word more than I meant to.

"Of course you do, they attack everyone."

He stood there, one hand on the open door. I opened my hands in front of me. "Please help me. Shay?"

In answer, he grabbed a coat off a peg and joined me outside. "My family are Christians, but their beliefs only go so far out of the norm. We'll need to talk outside."

"Haven't you told them you're a prophet?" I almost forgot my own distress.

He looked miserable. "What's wrong with your neck?"

All my horror came flooding back as I rubbed the crick in my neck. "I hurt it looking at the demon. It's on my shoulder blade, and I can't get rid of it." I ended on a whine; I felt helpless. But Shay would know how to fix it. He couldn't stop my seeing demons, but he would touch my shoulder and pray, and when I was able to move my neck to the left again, I would see nothing there.

We walked to a picnic table in the side yard. I sat on the table like I was at a doctor's office and turned sideways to show my left shoulder blade. But Shay stood with his hands in his pockets, chewing his lip. When he looked up at my face, he seemed resigned. I fought to keep my terror at bay.

"Well, can you pray for me?"

He nodded. He prayed. I took his hand to put it on my back, but he held my hand in his instead. It was warm. Silently, I prayed too, but it was more along the lines of "Please, please, please." I was picturing myself normal again. With normal people, doing normal things. A cold breeze blew against my face, and I squeezed his hand harder.

Still holding his hand, I twisted around, gasping twice as I forced my neck to turn. Two malevolent eyes stared back at me.

"It didn't work. It didn't work." Dropping his hand, I pressed my fingertips hard against my neck. I knew having a demon was worse, but the pain was excruciating. Shay didn't offer to massage it.

I calmed my breathing while I waited for the pain to subside. "Why haven't you told your parents? And are you really even a prophet? Isn't that just another way of saying you predict the future?" My tone sounded bitter, even to me. I felt diseased, broken. I didn't care anymore who else I hurt.

"A prophet is one who is given a message from God to his people," Shay said.

"But you don't have the message anymore."

"Well . . ."

My eyebrows shot up so high my neck ached again. "You remember it? What is it?"

"I can tell you the circumstances around it."

I had to focus directly on his eyes to avoid seeing the shapes of the demons diving and falling around him. He took off his jacket and draped it over mine. It had some woodsy, spicy scent to it, and the demons disappeared as my thoughts drifted.

"I was on the couch half asleep. Late at night. I had been restless for a week or more. Rose had just been admitted to the hospital. I ate, I read, I watched TV, I talked to my friends, but nothing satisfied this feeling that I was missing something. That night on the couch, I started to dream."

"Was it just a dream, or something more?" I hadn't meant to interrupt, but it popped out.

"It's possible that an ordinary dream can be used as something more than just a dream." He looked at me sternly, and I pressed my lips together as a promise to be silent.

"When I woke up from the dream, I saw snow falling outside. I ran out, barefoot. I felt the snow stinging my arms and face as the wind blew. I looked around to see if other people were outside to see it as well, but it was only falling in our yard." I must have looked skeptical—yes, me, the demon-seeing girl. He shrugged. "Yes, snow in Houston. I tried to take a picture, but my phone app wouldn't open. My parents and sister weren't home, and Rose was in the hospital. There was no one I could call to come over and see. I was standing by my mom's rose bushes, and right in front of me a red rosebud appeared, opened, and bloomed. The crystals of ice on the rose bush sparkled like diamonds under the porchlight." He looked at me like I wasn't getting it. "It's a white rose bush, El. A red rose on a white rosebush. I reached for it, and the petals fell and blew away." He sighed and looked away. "In a matter of minutes, the snow all melted, and the yard was simply wet."

Shay climbed onto the table next to me. "But the next day, I thought about the message in the dream, and talked myself out of it. Who was I to accuse someone? Especially with no proof. I knew that something miraculous happened, and that made me believe what I had heard was from God. But I had no proof for other people."

I was quiet a moment, taking it all in. "That wasn't the prophecy though, was it? What was in the dream?"

He took a deep breath and looked at his hands, flexing his fingers. "I have the memory of the first prophecy again, but this time I'm not allowed to tell the person it was intended for."

"Then tell me! Oh, wait . . ." I pointed to myself.

"No, it wasn't about you." He sighed. "It was very long, but the gist of it was, tell Jon Addison that if he continues on his current path, he will lose everything: his job, home, respectability, and he will lose it publicly. Everyone will know."

"Jon? Well, okay, knowing what I know now, that isn't a big surprise."

"Right, but imagine if you barely knew him and had to go tell him this."

"Yes, that would be . . . wait, you said the first prophecy? Do you have a new one? What is it?"

"I think the reason I forgot the first one till now was . . . not as a punishment exactly, but as a learning experience, because of my previous disobedience." He looked at me with a serious expression. "Because if you are told to do something and don't obey, then it's your responsibility."

Keeping my hand on my neck to give it more warmth, I settled more comfortably on the table. Would he massage his precious Rose's neck if she were sitting here groaning?

"Yeah, well, burden me."

"I was told to stay out of it."

"Out of what?"

"Everything. From now till after Christmas. Don't interfere. Let Eliana do what she needs to do." He raised a hand before I could speak. "I don't know what that is. I guess you'll know when you know. It's just that I can't do it for you."

We sat quietly for a few minutes. I could hear a small dog barking inside his house and sounds of a TV. One thing still bugged me about his story.

Softly, I said, "And it all comes back to Rose."

"What?"

"The miracle that proved that the prophecy was real—a rose blooming in front of you. It all revolves around her." A new ache in my gut was overshadowing my other pain, and I wasn't concerned with being nice. "And your 'incident' that caused you to leave college, that was probably Rose as well. You want to help her, and that is the only reason you took an interest in me."

He didn't look angry like I expected. "Eliana, other than the shopping mall, you keep coming to me. I'm not chasing you."

"I'm not chasing you either!" It came out more as a whimper because I moved my neck too fast, causing another whipcrack of pain.

"No, I didn't mean that—I meant, I think our paths are crossing for a reason. We can help each other."

"Do you want to use me to get to Rose or to bring down Jon? I saw the files he keeps in his office on his 'subjects,' but I also saw that he is losing it—like he is seriously becoming deranged. He has a huge demon on his back, and he's threatening to have me committed if I don't cooperate. And I came to you for help." I looked deep into his eyes and saw pain I hadn't seen there before.

"I will not use you, Eliana. But I don't think you will be free from all of this until Rose is." He raised a hand to my protest. "I don't make the rules. Sadly, I don't even follow them enough. I'm speaking from my own experience. I think you have been given a gift that will help people in a way that I can't."

"Then it's a stupid, annoying gift." Looking down at my hands, the words flowed out. "My father gave me a teddy bear for my tenth birthday. Mom was surprised because she had done all the shopping and decorating, and he went and bought an extra gift. A week later, I got home from school to find my mom, not crying, but rearranging the house to cover up the fact that Dad had taken a bunch of stuff and moved out. Like a hole was punched in my life and it was being papered over."

Shay put his arm on my back and patted it softly. Dimly, I imagined the demon being thunked on the head as he patted. "Your teddy bear is a gift, but also a reminder of a terrible day?"

Stopping myself from shaking my head, I sobbed once and took a breath. "The thing I remember most is how my brother looked at me when he got home. His birthday was a month later, but Dad was already gone."

My whole face felt wet. I rubbed it with my sleeves when my fingers weren't enough. He started to shiver, but if I pulled his coat off my shoulders, it would hurt my neck. *Am I being selfish?*

"Explain this to me, prophet. Why do I see the demons when I'm trying to understand other people, and when I'm being selfish and thinking of myself, then the sight is shut off?"

Shay crossed his arms over his chest, still shivering, and glanced back at the house. "What exactly do you see? What are the demons doin?"

His chivalry was admirable, but was getting silly. Keeping my left side immobile, I tugged at the coat with my right hand. "Here, take your coat." He stopped my arm, took the coat off me, and put it on.

"They grip onto people, on their faces, shoulders . . ." I grimaced. "Anywhere, really. It seems to be connected to what they are trying to do."

"And what's that?"

"They whisper to the people if they are near their ears, or they just grip tighter if they are elsewhere. I can't know that it's true, but I suspect that they each have a specialty. The people who gossip have them on their ear. If they are greedy, it's on their hand." He seemed interested.

Searching for the right words, I peeked up at the sky and was surprised to see stars. I hadn't thought it through this far, but it came to me. "I think that each one is working on their person to get them to do a certain thing, but I don't know what the end goal is."

"I guess when you're trying to understand other people, then you're open to seeing what's affecting them. When you're being selfish, you're blocking the input about other people."

I considered that, but was too tired to be sure I got it.

"What kind do I have?" He smiled, but I didn't think he was making fun of me. The sight was off finally, and I wanted it to stay that way, but I remembered how they had looked.

"All of them! Well, a lot anyway. But they don't seem able to hold on to you. I'm trying not to see them right now, Shay, it's upsetting."

"Sure." He looked up at the sky. "And what is yours?"

Holding back tears, I said, "It's pride. It must be. It looks like Jon's. His is on his back too. And he's not just arrogant, he thinks he's superhuman; that's why I think it's pride."

"Does that surprise you?" I must have given him a fierce look, because he went on hurriedly, "It surprises me. I don't think of you as prideful."

I thought about it. I didn't think of myself that way either, but does anyone see themselves the way they are? "I would have expected anger, I guess. I've been arguing with my mom a lot lately. And Susan at the studio makes me so mad with her nitpicking . . ."

"Maybe one, of whatever kind, attaches to us first, and it lets the others get in."

It was getting late, and my butt was sore on the cold wood of the picnic table. Shay hadn't done any magic to fix my problems, and apparently he couldn't even fix his own. I shifted my weight carefully and slid off the table to stand in front of him. He was looking at me strangely.

"What?" I replayed what he had just said. "Oh, no, Shay! You mean I might have more than one?" I wanted to just collapse on the ground and be done with it. Women in old movies used to faint all the time.

Shay stood too and patted my arm on the non-hurting side of my body. "Eliana, you will be fine. You are fine. The demons may give you a nudge, but they are not in control. No one is putting you away. You can do some good with your gift. But it's your choice."

The words burst out of me without any thought. "Shay, I'm tired of being hurt. Why would I risk more pain to help people I don't even know?" Tears filled my eyes. I couldn't say what was in my heart without risking my heart. I knew it as I stood there in front of him with his stupid messy hair that I wanted to touch and his eyes that I couldn't stop seeing even with my eyes closed. Why couldn't we just chat and laugh and go to a movie like normal people? Why did we have to meet this way? What I wanted to say to him was, what if I end up helping someone who will just take you away from me?

Shay said, "Eliana, you can risk pain because it's okay to be taken advantage of, okay to lose, okay to feel other people's pain—as long as you are giving willingly to the world. If you try to help the world and don't even make a dent, you've still done the right thing." The answer was outlandish to me, and for a moment I couldn't breathe.

"How can it ever be okay to be taken advantage of? How can that ever be right?" Shay looked at me steadily. "Why should I let that happen? And don't tell me 'because it's the right thing.' Where has the right thing gotten you?"

He touched the side of my face with just his fingertips. "I haven't done the right thing. I haven't done what I was told to do or what I already knew I should do. So I guess I can't tell you why." He put his hands in his coat pockets.

"Sounds like you're as useless as I am. I see and you hear, but neither of us does anyone any good." My words seemed to hurt him more than I expected. I stormed off as angrily as I could with a crick in my neck and a cramp in my butt.

***

Late that night, I cried, lying on the sofa bed with my neck cradled in every pillow and soft sweatshirt I could find. Plus a teddy bear.

I asked God: *Why did you even make me? What is the point? To worship you? You have better people for that. To look after others? I can barely take care of myself. I know I'm blessed, and I'm grateful, but you know, sometimes that makes it worse, because I feel like it's not okay to be unhappy.*

Bit by bit, my body finally relaxed. Thoughts, voices, or the beginnings of a dream, started in my head.

I thought, *I don't like getting involved in other people's problems.*

Another thought floated up, as if in answer, *Why not?*

I don't think I can be compassionate till I get my life sorted out.

You are a light in dark places. You give to people who are not able to give to you. I could hear the warmth in the voice, but I still felt unsure.

It's too messy, and I'm afraid.

What is there to fear? the voice asked.

I suppose, most of all, I'm afraid of being abandoned.

Darling one, was there ever a time you needed help and didn't get it? the voice asked.

I thought of my father, the unhappiness in my family. I hadn't asked for help then, though.

Eliana beloved, if you call out for help, one hundred angels will be there with you. Just take one step forward.

My eyelids wouldn't stay open. It was like I was having a conversation with someone else. Someone with a kind voice who cared about me. Although the room was dark, I had that same feeling as when I saw the sparkling light of the angels.

I drifted off to sleep, feeling the safest I had since I was ten.

22

Christmas Eve

The alarm clock clanged without mercy. It was still dark out. Darker than it should be. It was probably going to be a cloudy, miserable day, but it was too much trouble to keep checking the weather. Someone would let me know if a big storm was coming.

It had been just two days since all that craziness with Jon, Shay, and discovering my demon. I had forced myself to stop trying to look at my back, and my neck felt almost normal again. My lack of nightmares was noteworthy. As I climbed out of the sofa bed, Mariah burst out of her room and into the living room. "You're up! Finally! It's Christmas Eve!"

Oh dear Lord, when did she become a morning person? She was wearing new pajamas and a Santa hat and held a card and a candy cane.

"Yes, I have to go to work."

"Do you really have to go? They don't need everyone, do they?"

My feet were cold, and I couldn't find my socks. "Yes and no. They have enough people for elf duty, so I'm just going to be at the studio in case they need help—and for the party." Jim thought it would be more fair if we all went in, and he made it the day of our staff party.

"Maybe I should have planned to go."

"You'll have more fun at your family's house." Not surprising, since her foster sibs saw her as some kind of rock star.

"That's true. So, can we open presents now?"

We were both going to see family later that day. I would go to my mom's and she would go to her foster family's home, so we had agreed to exchange gifts that morning.

"Can I pee first?"

With great drama, she sighed and dropped onto my empty sofa bed. "Okay."

I swear I didn't take long, but when I got back she had already made the bed and tucked it away into the sofa. Her gift for me had appeared under our little tree, and the card and candy cane were hung on the tree's branches.

Mariah said, "El, I went to see what it was like outside, and you had a letter stuck on the door."

My brain was trying to process who would write a letter to me, let alone deliver it to the door. I went to the coat closet that doubled as my storage space and got her gift, then took the envelope from her. In a scrawl that managed to be both elegant and nearly unreadable, the face of it said, *"To Eliana."* I sighed as I took it.

Mariah still looked worried. "It was taped to our door. Who is it from?"

I ripped open the envelope and unfolded the paper. "The demon guy," I said while scanning the paper. It was a brief reminder that he would be filming at his office today and I had agreed to participate. He made it sound like an invitation to a really dull game night rather than a contract with the devil. Or one of the devils. I wondered if they all had the authority to sign deals, or was that only for *the* devil?

"Okay," she said, leaning over until she blocked my view of the paper, "I'm waiting to hear what the heck this is about."

"Well, don't judge me, but I agreed to let this guy hypnotize me . . ."

"Ew."

"I was just trying to get out of an uncomfortable situation at the time. I thought I would find a way out. But this is his reminder." I handed her the paper.

"Today? Why today?"

"Because the other 'subject' is on leave from the psych ward for the holiday, so it works for his schedule."

"Is that where you're going to end up?" Her tone said she was joking, but her face looked stunned when she saw whatever was on my face. "Oh, El. You're not crazy! What about that other guy, Shay? What does he say about this?"

"Oh, um, yeah . . . I kind of yelled at him the other night."

"But El, you like him. I can tell that you like a guy when you talk about him. Did you tell him how you feel about him?"

"How I feel? Mariah, no. Shay's too in love with the ex-girlfriend from hell." I smirked, thinking she would laugh, but she seemed taken aback. "There was nothing between us. I had thought maybe, but there's nothing on his end."

I tried to sum it up for her, "One guy is sweet and good and kinda weird and is messed up about his girlfriend in the crazy ward. The other is Mr. Grown-up, taking me to nice places and being suave, but he wants . . ." I groped for words, and realized it was my fear of admitting it that was holding me back. "He wants to experiment on me to learn more about demons." It was getting easier to tell her.

"He's threatening to put me in the crazy ward if I don't help him. Maybe even wants me to be possessed. I mean, he said he wouldn't do that to me, but how can I trust him?" I looked down at my hands. I felt better getting the words out, but they hung in the air like a cloud. Things can sound so simple out loud, but they're still not.

Mariah stared at me. "Oh my God El, do you hear yourself? You don't have to be with either of them. You only started seeing both of them because of the . . . the demons." It was the first time she had said the word to me. "If neither is helping you, dump them both. And if either is batshit crazy, then stay away."

"I don't think I can now." I saw the concern on her face. I smiled and patted her arm. "It's okay though. I'm in this, and I can handle it. I can't explain how I know this, but I know it will be fine. I just might not get everything I want, that's all. If I could help Rose, it would make Shay happy, although I may lose Shay if I help her. But I'm okay with it, really. And as for Jon"—I wadded up his note—"I'm just going to blow off his little event. He won't realize till it starts, then it will be too late."

I gave Mariah a quick hug, then picked up her gift from under the tree to change the subject. It worked—her eyes lit up.

I ripped the paper open, and she tensed. When I looked closer at the paper, I realized she had decorated it herself with ink stamps. I pulled the rest of the paper off without tearing it and set it down next to me. The gift was a photo album. I have a stack of them because people keep giving them to me. But this one made me pause. The cover said *"A Light in Dark Places."*

"Open it!" she insisted. It wasn't an empty photo album for me to use. It was full of photos. Selfies of the two of us. Some random photos of the apartment that I thought maybe were supposed to be artistic. And one of me, sitting on the couch, smiling mysteriously down at a small white business card in my hand.

"Thank you, Mariah." I gave her a hug, but I was still mystified.

I had taken the Bryce bag back to the department store to have it boxed and gift wrapped. The elegant wrapping paper seemed embarrassing somehow after Mariah's personalized paper. She opened it with great excitement. "Oh El, it's beautiful." Mariah looked at the tag hanging off the bag. "It's a Bryce." It was the tone of voice you use when you don't know what to say. She put it down quickly and hugged me.

Of course she oohed and ahhed over it. But I suspected that she was disappointed. I thought I knew her, of all people, but maybe I was wrong. Maybe I was wrong about everything. The photo album stayed in my lap like a puppy. I could feel the time and care she had put into it. The love. I understood why she had spent more time alone in her room lately. It was because she was spending time on my gift.

She bit her lip as she looked at the album again. "I wanted to try being the photographer for a change. And you were my model, you just didn't know it."

I laughed. "Next week I'll let you use my camera." Her face brightened. "Am I a light in dark places?"

"Yeah, you are." Mariah put her arm around my shoulders and looked me in the eye. "You're always there when I need you." I gave her a side hug, then let go to wipe a wet spot on my eye. She leaned the side of her head against mine. "I'm here for you too, El. I'm sorry about all you've been through lately."

***

Christmas Eve shopping at the mall was not as bad as I expected. Maybe most people were visiting relatives out of town. Or just, you know, organized enough to be done with their gift buying. My brother was not high on my list of priorities, but I felt like I ought to get him a gift. I went back to the same mega-department store where I had my "incident." I actually hesitated as I crossed the threshold. I made it to the men's accessories department, found gloves, and bought them without supernatural interference or EMTs. Awesome.

On my way out, I detoured through women's jewelry; a quick peek wouldn't hurt. Even the discounted prices reminded me I needed to watch my budget. I turned to go and saw a familiar figure hunched over the watch display.

The ex. Breaker of hearts and liar extraordinaire.

His hands were jammed into the pockets of his navy blue wool pea coat. Floppy dark hair fell over his wide forehead as he gazed into the display case. His pale face looked strained. I stared for a moment, too surprised to react. But of course he would be in town to visit his family for Christmas.

"Chas." The name slipped out. He didn't move, just kept staring at the watches. The sales lady walked up to him, carrying a bundle of keys.

"I'm sorry, we don't have that brand anywhere else. Just the ones you see here. Do you want me to get one of these out for you?"

He seemed relieved to have her there, but I walked over and stood by him, waiting to be seen. He tried again to ignore me.

"Uh, yes, let's see." His face was panicked as he looked at watches that obviously weren't the ones he wanted. "How about, maybe that one?" The sales lady tried her key, but it didn't work.

"Sorry, let me get the key for this display." She walked off and left him.

"Chas, seriously. Look at me."

He turned to face me. He was a terrible actor. "Oh, El, hi! I'm really busy now. The bag with my mom's gift got lost on the way here. I have to get a replacement and go."

"Uh huh." I could see the sales lady had been stopped by another customer. "How are you?"

He pulled his phone out and pretended to look at it.

"I threw out your stuff. Don't worry about having to get it." He actually met my eyes. "It's over and we're moving on." I took a breath and realized I wasn't nervous or angry or anything other than amused at his apparent fear at seeing me. "I'm sorry for anything I said or did, and I forgive you."

"You threw out my T-shirt?"

"Goodbye, Chas." I walked away, feeling lighter.

***

The studio was comfortable and familiar despite a new, additional layer of festive decorations. A group of photographers clustered around a photo booth, of all things, complete with holiday props. I stood with a pen poised over the group Christmas card to Jim, but my brain was jumping around so much I couldn't think of what to write.

The blank spot on Jim's card mocked me. How do you put all that someone means to you in a square inch of space, especially knowing that everyone else will read it too? I settled for *"Jim, you're the greatest! Merry Christmas!"* and signed my name.

Streamers and paper reindeer and snowflakes dangled from the ceiling. Susan must have stayed late the night before to do it all. Dozens of colorful canvas bags were piled under the tree, each with an employee's name laser printed across it. The mall planned to close early Christmas Eve so the studio was only open till noon for last-minute customers to duck in and pick up their photo orders. Santa Land had to stay open a little longer, so Jim decided to make it a party since someone had to be there anyway.

I went through the motions of getting a paper cup of punch and chatting with my fellow employees. Now, I thought, now is the time to get to know them. But most of the conversation revolved around their Christmas shopping, the great bargains they found or the elusive toy they couldn't get, or the parties they felt obligated to go to, and everyone mentioned how tired they were. I realized I had missed the important conversations when I was too busy to talk to them—how were their kids? Their spouses? Were they happy in their lives?

I walked to the back. I told myself I needed some quiet, that I wasn't used to so many people and so much noise in one room. But I was hiding. From them, and from my own inadequacy. I felt like I wasn't doing well with my family, I was becoming a stranger to my best friend, and my love life—forget about it. All I could think was that I was failing in so many areas of my life, and if I had to fake a smile and make small talk with coworkers who were still just strangers to me . . . well, I might scream.

I ducked into Jim's office and studio. Jim had a calming presence, even when he wasn't physically there. His desk was just messy enough to be comfortable. I sat in his chair, but I couldn't relax—I still felt weird about leaning back in a seat, knowing what was on my back. Instead, I put my head down on the desk. The party buzzed away in the front room. I couldn't get comfortable because of a book jutting out from a pile of crap and making the desk uneven under my elbow. I tried nudging it to the side, but it wouldn't move. I lifted my head to look at it just as Susan leaned in the doorway. "El, presents in five minutes." I nodded and sighed. I couldn't even put my head down without being disturbed. I jerked the book up from the pile. It was a Bible.

I found Daniel and looked for where I left off, but I saw this bit: *"My God sent his angel, and he shut the mouths of the lions. They have not hurt me, because I was found innocent in his sight. Nor have I ever done any wrong before you, Your Majesty."* That was no help to me. I couldn't say I hadn't done anything wrong. I was on the verge of tears when the party music volume dropped down. After dabbing my eyes, I rejoined the party.

To fill the time before presents started, I went to refill my empty paper cup. Susan was wiping up a spill on the drinks table. I heard that little thought-voice in my head say, *Go deeper.* I met Susan's eyes before she glanced away. *Ugh, I don't want to hang out with Susan at a party.* Intending to just cruise by her and keep walking as I talked, she looked up anxiously as I said, "Susan, the place looks great . . ." I trailed off as I saw a huge fly appear out of nowhere and start a lazy circle around Susan's head. "Uh, it looks fantastic; you must have worked really hard on this." I stopped, forcing myself to relax a bit and smile at her.

"Thank you, Eliana. I'm glad you like it." Her voice held steady all the way to the end and her eyes crinkled a little as she smiled.

"And how is . . . your husband doing?" *His name, what is his name?*

"Steve is doing better. We're glad he's home for the holidays." The fly disappeared into thin air as Susan's shoulders relaxed. I couldn't think of anything else to say that wouldn't sound forced. I held my hands apart for a second as a question, and she responded by reaching out to hug me. She smiled as I pulled away, and I stood still as she brushed a cookie crumb off my shoulder and smiled again.

I found a spot on the sofa to steady myself. I had thought I could turn my back on this stuff and get on with my life. Apparently, I couldn't. The party went on around me. Too much food, too many bright colors. The room seemed to shrink, and the laughter hurt my ears.

My purse and jacket were behind the counter, near the door, so I was able to leave without much fuss. Everyone was focused on the gift bags that were being handed out, and I could pick mine up next time I was there. I would tell Jim that I had more gift-wrapping to do, which was true. Mostly I needed to breathe.

***

My phone rang. For real. In a moment of boredom I had changed the ringtone to an old-fashioned clattering landline ring. The mall exit was just ahead, and I could be in the car in two minutes. I answered it without looking.

"Hello?"

"Eliana." Jon's voice was clear and businesslike. "We have an appointment. Are you on your way?"

The man was scary, but on the phone he was distant, safer. "Jon, I don't think I can . . ."

"El?" It was Mariah's voice. "Are you on your way home?" I froze. A man bumped into me and hurried on with an apology and a frown.

"Mariah? What's going on, where are you?"

"At home. Jon came by looking for you."

"Is he in the apartment?" I looked around for police officers, not sure what to even say to them.

She hesitated. "Yes."

I could hear the tension in her voice, and my stomach dropped. I angled the phone, trying to hide my rapid breathing. It was me he wanted; he would leave her alone if I played along. "Mariah, write down this number, right now, no questions." I had Shay's number memorized from all the times I started to text him, then didn't. She said she was writing it. "You got it? I want you to call that number as soon as he leaves."

She agreed. I considered my options while standing there in the middle of the mall. The crowds that had been pressing in on me physically and mentally for the past several weeks were finally dwindling as shoppers finished or simply gave up. I missed the comfort of being surrounded. I felt too alone. It left me with a single thought. A few miles away, thanks to Jon, a young woman I had never met was being held captive by a demon that had worked its way into her heart. And no one could see it but me.

"Tell Jon I'm on my way to his office now."

23

Trust

I parked by Jon's office building and turned off the engine. The overcast, midday light was weak, but the day would only get darker. I wasn't much for fly by the seat of my pants schemes, but I was out of time. I hoped Mariah would get some kind of help from Shay. His prophecy had said not to help me, but to "do what he was supposed to do." Maybe he could give Mariah some guidance. The brick building in front of me looked like a fortress against the gloomy sky. Shay's business card was once again in my pocket. On the back of it, in his neat print, was: *2nd Timothy—The Lord stood with me and strengthened me."* I needed that. A little voice in my head said, *Just take it one step at a time.*

The building was quieter than last time, with no cleaning crews anywhere. The light from Jon's office suite showed it was the only office occupied today.

At the office, people in matching black shirts and headsets were rushing back and forth with cables and lights. A woman with a clipboard raised her hand to me as if to send me away, but her face registered recognition. "Eliana, right?" I nodded, my hand still on the office door. "The crew is setting up now. I'll take you in." I was speechless, but she didn't seem to notice as she bustled over to show me the way. "Don't be nervous, there's a handheld camera cruising around to get behind-the-scenes footage as well as the main camera. Just pretend it isn't there."

I followed her toward a conference room and heard Jon's voice from beyond a set of double doors. I wasn't ready. "Oh, can I drop my purse in Jon's office first?" She looked hesitant, so I said, "I know where it is. It'll just take me a minute." Another crew member came up to ask her something, and I turned without waiting for a response.

I turned on the light in his office. Instead of gathering my wits and figuring out my next step, I was distracted. A group of photographs was on the wall to my right, tacked up with pushpins. The subjects seemed to be in their mid-teens to early twenties. The bottom row all had X's over them in black marker. I moved closer.

Each had a name and a word or two at the bottom.

Marcus, committed.

Angela, relocated.

Miriam, lost.

Scott, dead.

All but one on the next higher row were crossed out. Only Rose remained.

One more row sat at the top, but there were only question marks next to those names.

Andrew, ?

Jill, ?

Eliana, ?

My photo showed me sitting by the swimming pool, reading, with my keys in one hand. It had the flat look of a picture taken with a telephoto lens. That's why the woman outside had recognized me.

I took a step back. Who were these people? How many others had Jon already gotten his claws into?

I leaned against the desk. *I can't do this, how can I rescue anyone? He's too powerful and . . . evil. I'm alone, all alone.* Why did I think I could do anything just because I see people's demons?

I wasn't going to risk another crick in my neck to look, but I could sort of sense the little demon on my shoulder. Pride? Was I being arrogant about something? Why wasn't it just anger? The pink frou-frou girl in the studio and the rage in her eyes as she talked about her ex flashed through my mind. She had a burned, flaky demon on the middle of her back. I felt around inside my head for what might be the anger demon and felt a scuttling sort of nothingness, like when you just miss seeing a bug fleeing into a crack in the wall. I searched deeper and sensed the panicky feeling darting around. Yes, that one was still on me too.

My attention shifted back to the pride. How did those two team up? I thought of how angry I was at my mom for going on with life like my dad never existed. How Chas became evasive as we got close to Thanksgiving and didn't tell me he had made new plans that didn't include me. How he lied.

I lie too.

It hit me in the gut. I wanted to argue against it, rationalize what I do. But there it was. *Yes, I do lie—to myself as well as to others. I'm not proud of it, but it's true.* Chas was a way to run away from home as much as he was someone to be with. The anger caused me to blame other people, and the pride said I was better than they were. A weight lifted. Not the demons, but I felt better. I wasn't trying to fight it anymore.

I found my voice and said out loud, "When I was sad, you said you are with me, so I know you are here." I looked around—no one appeared. I turned toward the door, to the foyer and the fear that lay beyond it.

One step at a time . . .

It was a supreme effort, but I took one step forward, and before my foot touched the ground, a hundred angels had joined me, all marching with me. I don't know how I knew it was a hundred, I just trusted that it was. They didn't seem able to stay in formation—most broke off, circling around, zooming so fast they were mere flickers of light in the room. At my side was one angel I could focus on, moving at a human pace. His face was almost solid looking, like it was made from Mariah's iridescent glass tree ornaments. I hesitated with my hand on the door handle.

He smiled at me. "I love you." I recognized his voice as the one I'd heard while falling asleep.

"Thanks." I was uncomfortable. "But you don't even know me."

"Oh, but you're wonderful. You're just like He said you would be, long ago, before time."

"Wait, are you talking about God?" My voice dropped to a whisper on his name, and I cleared my throat. "He saw that I would be a mess like this, and he made me anyway?"

"Mess? You are amazing. You are not a mess."

"I'm here to rescue a woman from a demon, and I have no idea how to do it. I don't even have Bible verses memorized to use." I thought of all the things I had failed at or done halfway in my life. "I'm kind of a loser."

He seemed to see what was in my head. He smiled and shook his head, throwing more shimmers of light around me. "Those things—those are not your life's work."

"So what is?" I was eager to know.

"You will find out, one step at a time."

Memories swirled in my brain of smiling at people, patting a hand or back, encouraging someone who was nervous in front of the camera and helping them relax. "But," I said, disappointment heavy in my voice, "that's nothing."

A memory of Mariah sitting with me while I cried about Chas. He was not important to me now, but I remembered the pain at that time and how much it meant to me to have her there, just listening. Just patting me on the back. Everything I needed.

I mulled it over as I slipped out the door and across the foyer to the entrance to the conference room they were using for filming. One last crewman entered the room ahead of me, and I waved him on when he started to hold the door for me.

I stared at the double doors to the conference room. I could hear a muddle of voices inside, then suddenly, Jon's voice boomed out, "She's here? Where is she? Bring her to me!"

Something began moving on the crack between the doors.

A small black something crawled onto the front of the door, then another, then three more. They tensed and spread their wings as Jon's voice continued to thunder inside, giving orders. The swarm of fear flies rose into the air and arced down, right toward my face. I stood my ground. They slowed and began their horrible, silent circling around my head.

"Eliana"—the kind voice of the angel was behind me—"the Bible verses are not what you need now. God has given you a gift and the power to use it. He works through you." I turned around, but I couldn't see my angel friend clearly anymore, just the shimmers of light that danced off him. One fly, then another, swooped closer to my face, making me flinch. The voice grew warmer, kinder. "You have a choice, Eliana. You have learned a lesson and have shown you have the courage to face your enemy. I can take the visions away now. You can be like everyone else again."

An argument started inside me. *Why on earth would I stay this way for one more minute?* But the other side of me, the strong and confident side, answered out loud, "I'm keeping it. I want to do more."

I pushed the doors open with both hands and stepped into the room. The fear flies dropped to the floor around me. I saw the ones on the left flatten out, as if stepped on by an invisible pair of feet.

At the other end of the room a fake living room had been created. It looked alien in this large room, dark in the corners but brightly lit over the sofa, comfy chair, and artificial background plants.

I strode toward the set with my swirling entourage. Jon was preparing by the sofa. I figured he would be surprised at my companions, then remembered I was the only one in the world who would see them. Even if someone else out there had the sight, it wouldn't work through the cameras.

Jon dusted off some excess face powder as he talked to a camera operator. "The first one has a different type of information. She can see, but not hear. But she will be useful . . ." The camera operator nodded toward me.

I stood before Jon, still shaking. *Why am I scared when I know I'm protected?*

God never promised you a happy ending, Eliana, the thought floated up, *only that he would be with you—maybe he'll be with you in death too.* I couldn't decide if this was my regular fears or the angelic good voice. It was simply true, not good or bad. I didn't know how this would end. It wasn't exactly a comforting thought, but I felt calm. The flickering angelic lights swirled and disappeared. One of the last to leave brushed past Jon's face, and only I knew why he shivered.

He looked me up and down with a lazy sort of interest. "Well, you kept your word and came to participate."

"I'm here to save Rose."

He laughed. "Why? She is nothing to you. And you'll lose your little churchy boyfriend in the bargain."

"Because it's okay to be taken advantage of, to lose, to feel other people's pain—if you are giving willingly to the world. If you try to help and don't even make a dent, you've still done the right thing."

"That's crazy."

A man in a white uniform chimed in, "We don't use that word."

Jon dismissed him, "This is Texas, and crazy is crazy."

I took a closer look at the man in white. He was weightlifter-level bulky with sharp eyes. Like a security guard, bouncer, or . . . maybe a hospital orderly. Rose must be around. Jon snapped his fingers. "Tony, get to work. Miss Eliana mustn't leave the room till we're finished." Tony tightened his biceps like it was a reflex and headed toward me.

Tony guided me firmly to a seat on the sofa. According to his name badge, he was a paramedic. Was he there for extra medical help or just to transport Rose? Two crew members came out of nowhere to powder my face and smooth my hair. Another adjusted lights for my position.

Jon disappeared in the glare of the lights, then reappeared nearby, hovering in front of me. I realized my vision had clicked off. I turned it on. It was a relief at this point, like I had been holding back what was natural.

The green demon's head was perched on Jon's shoulder now, unafraid of my seeing it, with its cheek tight against his skin. In fact, rather than show fear, it sneered at me. It held my gaze as first one green claw, then the other, came into view. The head was not merely in front for the view; the demon was keeping its hold and balance by gripping Jon with its neck to free up its claws.

Looking at the demon, I said, "I will get rid of you."

Jon sighed. "You don't know when to quit, do you little girl?" He barked at the crew to take a break and told Tony to go with them. With a confused look at us both, the makeup people dusted me off and headed out a side door with the other crew.

I would have been offended by Jon's arrogance if I weren't so fascinated by what I saw. As the claws came around to the front, they glided down Jon's arms. The longest claw on each side touched Jon's wrists as if to puncture the skin. Instead, they melted as if they were smoke, and the clawlike hands disappeared into Jon's hands.

So smooth; it's like it's done it a thousand times.

My thoughts were cut off as Jon grabbed me by the throat and drew me closer. His eyes seemed as stunned as I felt.

"I will get what I want." One eye twitched, and beads of sweat popped on his forehead. The demon face was so close I expected to feel its breath, but there was none.

I inhaled sharply. *I can breathe, but how?* I risked a downward glance. Another hand grasped Jon's wrist, preventing a full range of motion. A glowing, translucent hand . . .

"I will cast you out." I looked at the demon as I said it. Might as well give it a laugh. And it did laugh, but it was only a quick movement of its lips, and then it was back on task.

Jon dropped me with a dismissive shove and stepped back. I gathered myself for whatever would follow. His eyes darted around. The demon was whispering into his ear like a huge frog flapping at a fly.

Jon mouthed the words silently first, then found his voice. ". . . keep trying . . . will find the way to get what I want . . . can't use them without being inhabited. And if you are inhabited along the way, oh well. I've seen so many teens damage themselves . . . I don't see why one more matters."

The demon's head pulled up and back, behind Jon again. I was hopeful that it had retreated, but then it pushed into Jon's head as smoothly as the claws had entered his hands. I saw the shift in Jon's eyes. At first glance they might look calm, but they were more like dead. Like a shark's eyes.

The eyes studied me. "You're not as pretty as I thought you were. And so much trouble."

Finally, horribly, the demon pushed further inside him. The last of the green head vanished, and Jon's voice deepened and roughened. The demon was in his head, controlling him. His face was cruel and cold.

I had to work quickly. Even though I'd come to help Rose, I didn't want Jon's demon to make it all the way to his heart. He could do too much damage, even without her to help him.

"Tell me your name."

He scoffed. "What do you want with that?"

"If you're not afraid of me, then tell me your name."

Jon drew himself up taller and smacked his chest with one demonized hand. "I am Pride."

I wasn't sure what to say next; I was not pleased to meet him.

"Everybody wants the same things, Eliana. You're not special; you're not different from anyone else."

That burned in my chest. Why? I felt my own pride. In fact, I became keenly aware of it, and realized why it had been so hard to let go of my anger. I wanted to be the one who was right, the one who got sympathy, the special one. As I stared down into my soul, I saw that my pride didn't need to be ripped out of me or off of me, but I just needed to let go of it. If I could just be okay with being humbled in front of others—even if they all thought I was stupid, wrong, messed up, inferior, crazy, not good enough–then I could choose how to be happy in any circumstance. What other people thought didn't matter. I had an angel who thought I was wonderful.

"Amazing anyone would love me, isn't it? But God does. He does, and I'm learning to love myself." He looked perplexed. *Good, he's hesitating. Now I have to finish him.*

I wanted witnesses. Without thinking, I yelled. "Okay, break's over! I'm ready for my interview!" With a sweet smile at Jon, I settled onto one side of the sofa.

The crew trooped back in. Jon, looking venomous, sat on the other sofa cushion. He pulled tidy notecards out of his jacket pocket, but I could see they were blank. It was all for show. Well, I was ready to perform.

"Get the camera rolling. We'll add the introductions later," he growled. The crew obeyed. They avoided interacting with him as much as possible.

At the director's cue, Jon gave me a smarmy smile. "Eliana, how long have you been seeing these . . . visions?"

I looked straight into his hollow eyes. "A few weeks. But my gift has been growing fast."

A hint of a real smile touched his lips. "Excellent. How would you like to maximize your gift, right now?"

I smiled warmly. "That sounds wonderful."

His brows creased momentarily, then he forced a pleasant look as he pulled a pen out of his pocket. "I can do that for you; you merely have to relax and concentrate."

"Oh, I don't even have to do that." I was hurting my cheeks with that smile. "My gift comes from God, and his love gives me all the power I need."

Jon stared blankly at me, still holding the pen up in front of my face. The director whispered, "Do you want to start again?"

My smile faded, my lips still open. My left arm twitched slightly. My shoulder moved. I said quietly, "Watch me love someone."

I fell to the floor, faking the fit that I had at the store. Jon stared at me, dumbstruck. I waved my arm erratically and arched my back painfully. I concentrated like it was a dance. First one part of my body, then another. Though I couldn't see it, I felt the pride demon fall off me.

I heard a walkie-talkie come to life behind me and Tony's voice said, "Charlie, do you read me? Seizure in a guest."

A staticky voice answered. I tuned it out. Right arm, face, back, legs . . .

Tony the paramedic appeared in front of my face. I had to jerk my head away to avoid thinking of Shay's concerned face at the store. Jon, somewhere behind Tony, yelled at him, "Leave her alone, she's not your problem!"

A car horn honked three times outside, and I almost lost my concentration.

Jon had probably counted on the holiday to keep people out of the building, but that only applied to regular visitors. Not to pizza delivery guys.

He looked up to see the production assistant leading in Dylan, the last member of "The Team" that I'd met. He was carrying a stack of pizza boxes. So that's what Dylan's evening job was. Jon's eye began to twitch. Dylan spoke in a monotonous patter, "That's two supremos with extra cheese, one pepperoni glutton, and a veggie platter pie." The crew seemed happy for the first time as Dylan set the pizzas down.

Jon shouted at them, "Leave it! I want this place locked down. No one comes in." I was only twitching now—fake seizures will tire you out. Jon glanced at me resentfully, then waved his arms at the crew. "I am paying double your normal salary today and I want obedience. This facility is locked down."

The camera operators pulled back from the pizza at the mention of salary and started readying for another take. The handheld camera was already rolling. But Mariah came strolling in next with a small boombox. High heels and a touch of body glitter jazzed up her elf costume and green tights. She struck a pose and announced, "Someone has sent you a Singing Elf Christmas Gram!"

The production assistant shrugged at Jon and mouthed, "Sorry."

Another paramedic, who I thought must be Charlie, appeared and put a towel under my head and moved away, maybe for pizza; I wasn't judging. *If there are two of them here, is Rose alone someplace?* I heard a soft voice that said, "Don't ask it to come out; tell it to come out. Not with pride in yourself, but be humble and let Jesus do what you can't." Up to that point, I had thought I was being daring, but I had to go further. I wasn't going to hint or ask for it, but demand that it leave. I remembered Major, holding that broken bottle and threatening my would-be abductor on a lonely street.

Jon leaned over me. This was my chance. I reached up and grabbed his face. I felt revulsion flow from my hand to my toes like an electric shock, but I held on. Jon's face contorted with fury, and his mouth opened in a yell that never came, because I spoke first.

"Pride demon! Get out of him!" He didn't even blink. I curled my body up to get my face right into his. His breath smelled like metal. "You are a demon from hell. In the name of Jesus Christ, you leave this man!"

He slowly rolled his eyes. It was like slow-motion sarcasm. I didn't know what else to do—put my hand on his forehead? But as I watched, his eyes continued rolling slowly up till his lids drooped and I could only see the whites. His whole body collapsed like the bones were gone, and I scuttled to the side for safety. One final shudder, and he lay still. I thought for a moment he was dead, it was so silent, but then I heard him take a breath. I couldn't see anything on his back. I closed my eyes halfway and put my head back down.

Charlie came running back, a slice of pizza in his hand, and saw Jon on the floor. "What the hell . . . ? Mr. Addison?" Jon sat up, saw the handheld camera in his face, and scrambled to his feet. He seemed dazed but suspicious as he looked back at me. I twitched some more.

I could hear Mariah chatting up the crew; it sounded like she knew two of them from a music video she had been in. The lights were obscured as Dylan leaned over me. *Oh, don't blow it, please . . .*

"El, uh Miss, are you okay? Can you hear me?" Dylan asked.

"Miss, are you on any kind of medication?" Charlie was trying to take over, probably accustomed to useless, panicky family members.

Dylan was looking curiously at my movements now. Charlie looked at Dylan, and I took the opportunity to murmur, "Suuuurffff," before going back to looking dazed. Dylan put a hand over his mouth.

"Is she a friend of yours? Do you know anything about her condition?"

"She goes to my church." Dylan had recovered his composure. "She's not on medication." His mind was working, but would he be fast enough? "She had a seizure once before, but she was fine afterward. She just . . . sees demons on people." The truth could work here. Why not? It was the reason for the whole video shoot.

Meanwhile, Jon was vomiting nearby. "She's crazy," he coughed, "she tried to kill me." He was probably transitioning from demon-related illness to just ticked off that he was about to lose his livelihood. Tony stood near him with his arms crossed, ready for any actual emergency, but not too concerned about Jon.

The two paramedics had a quick discussion on whether to call me an ambulance or let me have a little time to recover here. Dylan's reassurances helped them decide that, since I'd had a seizure before and wasn't under treatment, they would just put me in a quiet place for now. Dylan knelt by me once more and whispered, "Shay's not coming. He said this one is all yours. You'll know what to do." I relaxed.

"Dylan, tell Mariah I need to be alone with Rose. If I can get to her, you two keep everyone away from us."

I saw Dylan go to Mariah and speak very fast into her ear. My tigress friend was going to have to trust us both. I was afraid to risk winking at her, but she winked at me and nodded her head. Her hands were still clasped in front of her chin, though.

Tony produced a lightweight wheelchair and helped me into it. He wheeled me toward the door.

"Hurry back! We'll wait till you get back for the Singing Elf Gram!" Mariah called out. Tony looked back over his shoulder, and she waved cheerfully at him.

My last view as the conference room doors closed was Mariah and Dylan standing close together and bowing their heads.

The door clicked hollowly as it shut.

<h1 style="text-align:center">24</h1>

Finding Rose

I guessed that if Jon was going to film Rose, then she would be prepared and waiting in another room "offstage." The quick appearance of the second paramedic had told me it was close by. I shut my eyes against the nausea that was arising as I went forward with the plan. The plan that I didn't know any part of.

Beep.

I peeked out of one squinted eye. Charlie moved ahead and disappeared around the corner.

Tony asked, "Are you feeling better?" I squeezed my eyes shut again.

"Mmmhmm." But I said it in the weakest murmur I could. Tony was careful to wheel me slowly. I was surprised at the patience. I'd expected them to simply drop me in the first quiet place they found. If they were fully responsible for Rose, any time spent with me was outside of their concern.

A familiar sound was pecking at me, requesting my attention. I was safe, and so was Jon, though he wouldn't consider losing his business a good thing. But there was something else I was supposed to do—*listen, listen.*

Beep.

It was louder. I squinted my eyes open and saw Charlie exit a room and close the door with a concerned look at me. He gave the door handle an extra tug. Tony wheeled me past, and I heard another beep, muffled by the door on my right.

Rose.

It was her "beeper." The one that let staff know where she was at all times when she was out of her normal area, because they thought she was surprisingly cunning and resourceful for a young girl and too good at escaping.

"I need . . ." I tried to wilt. "I need to sit still . . . please." Tony seemed compassionate and patient; maybe he would respond to politeness.

"We'll get you to a room and you can lie down."

The beeping became softer again as they passed the door. Wilting more, I looked up at him.

"I think I'm going to be sick . . . now. If I could just be still." It couldn't work. Surely he had encountered all sorts of manipulation in his time—mentally ill doesn't mean stupid. Still, his uniform was so white and clean.

I managed a small "urp" for emphasis.

"It's just here," he said, pulling me to an open doorway. It was a small interview office with four chairs, a table, a phone, and a leather upholstered bench.

Beep.

He lifted me and set me on the bench before I knew what was happening. Mental note: no point fighting this guy physically. A flutter of hopelessness hit my stomach. *What can I do?* That was when I noticed the keys on his belt. What if Rose's door was locked? How would I open the door?

Quick, ask for something, something they are willing to get, but have to leave me alone for. And leave Rose alone for. Once he left me, he might take her out to film with Jon. Just because he was de-demonized for the moment didn't mean he wasn't still a self-centered opportunist. But my mind was blank. *I'm blowing it, I'm blowing it. Look up.*

I obediently looked up and met Tony's gaze. He was studying my face. *I've got nothing. Nothing.* His face softened.

"Better? Do you need a garbage can, or can you make it to the bathroom?"

"I just need to rest a few minutes," I said, pleading with my eyes. "Besides, you two will miss all the pizza and the Singing Elf if you stay back here."

Beep.

He looked at me uncertainly, probably weighing the liabilities if I got hurt somehow.

"I'm going to leave you here. Just for a few minutes. Put your head down if you need to." He ducked out the door, then came back with a small plastic trash can. He set it at my feet then darted out.

I kept up the sick charade another moment in case he came back. I tried to slide quietly off the couch, but it squeaked with every movement. I hesitated, but didn't hear footsteps. I did hear Jon shouting in the distance. Apparently, he wasn't feeling grateful about his newfound spiritual freedom. Did he even understand what happened? *Some people are stubborn. And that includes me.*

I crept into the hallway, ready to look sick if anyone saw me. I listened for a moment at Rose's door. I didn't hear anyone else talking, so I had to hope for the best. To my relief, the door handle turned. It was dark inside, so I felt around and found the light switch.

A quick glance gave me the impression of another conference room with a meeting table and chairs at one side and a lounge area at the other, but with something odd, out of place . . .

Beep.

Real nausea crept into my stomach. Casually, I turned toward the sound.

The end of the room was a cozy nook. A well-stocked bookcase and a lamp table flanked an overstuffed purple sofa.

Beep.

In the middle of the sofa, an emaciated girl sat like a queen on her throne. A force emanated from her, as if light were coming from her skin, like she was reaching her arms across the room toward me. I pulled back without meaning to.

Taking a breath, I opened up to see them. But I was already open. No demons showed up; just the odd girl, now grinning at me, the skin of her face stretching tightly across her bones.

"Shay says 'Hi.'" It was awkward, but the silence was making me uneasy. Jon's shouting would have been better. I tried again to see demons. I couldn't see anything, but I could feel it. That "not right" feeling was flowing across the room. Warning me.

"There is nothing for you here, Eliana-Who-Sees-Us." Her voice was not girlish, but reedy and harsh.

I straightened up. "You know my name. What is your name, Demon?" I looked as hard as I could. Where could it be? She was too thin to be hiding a major demon behind her.

Rose responded. Or rather, it did. Her body tensed up and her chest pulled forward as if on a string. A dark shape pulsated in Rose's chest, as if she were being X-rayed, and Rose's hoarse voice croaked out, "I am Bleakness . . . soul famine. The soul pines and I watch it starve."

Rose continued to stare at me, teeth exposed in a grimace-like smile. Like a spider contemplating a fly that is just out of reach. "Why have you come?" she asked.

"I want you, Rose, to go home. I want them gone."

Rose laughed. It was like the sound of metal scraping on pavement. Then her voice returned to the reedy sound. "Rose will die here. I will leave aching holes in many lives when I go, creating openings for more of my kind to worm their way into new homes. You cannot change that; it is hopeless."

"I'm here because I can see what others can't. And I won't leave until Rose is free."

Again, the laugh. "You will be diagnosed as insane. You would abandon everything you care about? For a woman who is your competitor in love? Why?"

An image of Shay sitting on the picnic table outside his house popped into my head. Tears threatened, but I fought them back.

Rose's face took on a bored look. A bored puppet.

"Even Jon cannot help you. He thought he could use us like circus animals. We allowed it. He reaped the benefits and did not notice when he crossed the line and began using the ones we inhabited." The lips pulled up into a smile as the hands touched Rose's chest. "We did his bidding and waited for the opportunity to use him. It came when he met you."

"Me?"

"He asked for help to attract you. We gave up a favored subject to gain his cooperation."

That didn't make sense until I remembered how happy he was to tell me that my would-be abductor had been found dead. He had asked his "associates" to look into it. I wrapped my arms around my ribs to stop a shiver.

Rose smiled with her puppet face. "We wanted you more. No one is to see us. No one must know of us."

"Then you made a bad choice in allowing Jon to create a video."

"We have no concern regarding Jon. He cannot harm us. You have no power over us, either. This is your own personal hell, Eliana-Who-Sees-Us. If you attack us in this body, they will think you are unstable and violent, and you will be locked up in a place like this girl is. You will be trapped. Everything you hate and fear. You will not be able to escape your mother, or men like Jon . . ." My mouth went dry. I took a hard breath. She tilted her head with a jerk. "You can see what torments you, unlike the others there. There is no hope for you. You have nothing to look forward to if you win and release the girl. And you have less than nothing if you lose."

She smirked at me. I wanted to hit her, but it wasn't Rose saying any of this. My hurting her would only delight her "inhabitant" even more. I felt that scuttling sensation in my head again. My demon? Anger?

I realized I had heard this demon before, telling me there was no hope. It was the same dark voice that had spoken to me so many times, pulling me down, discouraging me. But this time, I didn't feel the same. Despite myself, I smiled. The demon, Bleakness, turned cautious.

"Hope is alive and well. And where is my demon?" I waved toward my shoulder, as if showing it to her. I didn't need to hurt my neck this time. I had learned to sense it. "Pride is gone. And thank you for helping me find the anger demon."

I knew I could do it now, without knowing how I knew. I took a slow breath. In my mind's eye, my anger demon shrank and slid down, losing its grip. I shivered and "saw" it drop off me, tiny teeth grinding.

I moved toward Rose, who tried to crawl backward into the sofa. I held both hands out toward her. Palms up, like I was beckoning her toward me. Closer. "His power is within me. With his help, I can do this."

"No, no . . ." Rose pulled back and turned her head to the side. She was like a toddler now, being faced with strained carrots or bedtime.

I took another step forward. Rose turned on me again like a cornered animal. Baring her teeth, she growled. I was so close now. I bent forward.

"Touch me and they will think you are attacking me. Touch me and they will put you away for good." With a triumphant sneer, Rose pulled the wire from her tracker up in front of her face and yanked it off. A high-pitched alarm droned from her armband. A similar alarm could be heard down the hall. "Too late, witnesses will . . ."

I grabbed both sides of Rose's face, puckering her lips out and obliterating any warning about what the witnesses would do.

"Bleakness, you will leave. By the power given to me by the Lord, I order you to leave in the name of Jesus."

Her back arched, and her face looked terrified and pained. I stepped back, fearing I was hurting Rose, but this had to be done. Was I doing it wrong? Doubt crept in as Rose howled in real pain. No more doubt now. I held my palms out toward Rose. She clawed at her chest and gasped for air.

Then her body went limp, and I bent to help her. I pulled back again in disgust. A demon head stuck out from Rose's sternum, over her heart. It was blind, with only dark, pinched flesh over its eye sockets. Its face held a horrible expression, as if it had been frozen in mid-scream, showing tiny, sharp teeth. A small arm flailed out from Rose's chest, then the other. The weight of these two appendages tipped the balance, and the rest of the body slid out like a slug. It writhed and slid down to Rose's belly. I stood still, mouth gaping. It was already trying to expand itself out into a dark cloudlike shape.

Send it away, the angel's voice said, *it has no more power over either of you. Unless you let it back in.*

"No!" I pushed my palms toward the disgusting thing. "In the name of Jesus, I order you to leave."

With a boom, the overhead lights flashed and died, and a window exploded outward, showering glass on the lawn as the demon flung itself from the room. I shivered. My body continued shaking. My adrenaline was flowing with no place to go.

I jumped onto the couch next to Rose. Patted her cheeks. "Rose? Please wake up, please wake up."

They're going to come for you, a small voice in my head threatened. *They're coming now, and they'll think you hurt her.*

Rather than resist, I agreed and said, "Fine, they can lock me up —it was worth it." The voice vanished. Rose opened her eyes. She seemed bewildered as she looked at me as if for the first time.

When the paramedics and director ran in, we were huddled together on the couch. Everyone expected me to still be sick, not ecstatic. Rose spoke up first, "What was that?" We didn't have to fake our wide eyes or anxious expressions.

Everyone seemed suspicious, and while Tony gave me a cursory examination, the crew filmed the room and looked in vain for any object that could have broken the window and bent the metal grillwork outside it, but nothing was found. Since we had no cuts on us, they knew we couldn't have done it barehanded.

25

Home

I walked back into the main conference room, and I felt cold inside. I felt around in my mind and my gut; it didn't feel like a demon on me, so why was I so afraid? *Oh, right, that.* Would Shay still want anything to do with me with Rose freed? I locked eyes with Dylan and my stomach tightened. He and Mariah ran to me. Their faces were joyful. I wished Dylan was just glad to see me, not running over to get news of Rose for Shay.

Before hitting me like a freight train, Dylan grabbed my arms and spun me around. "Eliana!" We all nearly fell over as Mariah joined in for a group hug. "Are you okay?"

"She's going to be fine." I said. "Rose's demon is gone now."

"But El—can I call you El? I want to know how you are." His face was so serious. I wondered how he put up with those other goofballs.

After a second's hesitation, I smiled. "Dylan, I'm fine." I added a small laugh.

Mariah just stood with her arms around me, like she was going to lose control and sob if she spoke. I patted her arms and didn't try to push her away.

Trying to sound like a medical professional, I said to Dylan, "Tell Shay I did what I came here to do. Rose is safe now. Nothing and no one is making her seem ill now, so the doctors will have to release her soon." My gut was telling me to stop, to not do this. But it seemed logical to make a clean break. And now was as good a time as any.

"Once her parents hear the truth, Shay will be able to be with her again." Should I shake his hand to make it final? I reached forward, but he was standing as still as a stone. I patted his arm. "Um, well, I'll see you around. I guess."

"You're saying goodbye? You're not going to join us on The Team?"

I felt Mariah stiffen as she listened.

My small, forced laugh only highlighted the silence around me. "Maybe we can talk shop sometime. Demons, angels, whatever . . ." His buoyant manner drained, and I had to turn away.

I grasped for something to say. "Mariah, you have to get to your family. We should go."

She looked from me to Dylan and back, her brow creased like there was a joke she didn't get. "Uh, yeah. I do need to go."

Dylan nodded. He shook hands with the remaining crew members, gave a quick hug to Charlie, who was still hovering nearby, then waved, unsmiling, at Mariah and me. He looked dumbfounded, but didn't protest as he left.

Mariah grabbed my arm as he went out the door. "What are you doing? Are you possessed?" Her face was inches from mine. "I'm sure Shay loves you, not Rose."

Her words thrilled me, but I resisted. "But Rose is his girlfriend. Even if he's interested in me—and he's not—it's kind of icky to dump your girlfriend while she's in a mental hospital with a demonic possession."

"Okay, yeah—if it's true. But who told you they were an item? Dylan's been telling me that he and Rose were in love. Shay and the rest are just friends with her."

I stopped trying to pull back and just stared at her. I turned to look at the living room set. Jon was holding his head and muttering to Charlie about taking a cab home and sleeping it off. They both looked up to see my toxic glare.

Mariah followed my gaze and gave me a sympathetic look as she let go of my arm. The idea of having to ask Shay how he felt about me made me feel queasy. I just couldn't. Then I felt the scratchy feeling of Pride trying to get back into place. "Oh, I hate this, but I'll have to talk to Shay. Just not tonight." Mariah gave me a look. "Okay, tonight," I said and pulled out my phone.

I listened to my gut this time and typed, *I made a mistake. Can we start over? I need to talk to you.* I showed it to Mariah and hit send.

We walked out to the parking lot. She was all packed up and ready to go to her family's house. She didn't like to leave me alone, but I promised I would grab clothes and go straight to my mom's. We hugged like people who were saying goodbye forever. My phone chimed and we both jumped. Shay's reply was, *"After Christmas."* I gave Mariah a grim look.

She smiled at me. "Have faith, El."

***

The door to my mom's house had a new wreath on it, but the doorknob was the same pitted brass that had been on it since we moved there. You had to turn it just right to get it to open, like a secondary defense against would-be burglars. I stood a long moment before I got my key out. I wasn't the same person who had walked out this door a few weeks ago.

My mom was happy to see me. I dropped my duffel bag of dirty clothes on the floor and gave her a long hug. We didn't talk about Thanksgiving, but went on as if it had never happened. After dozing off that night during a Christmas movie and then tottering off to my old bedroom, I woke in the morning feeling more rested than I had in months.

My brother and sister-in-law came over, carrying shopping bags of gifts and a broccoli casserole. They kissed and hugged me and "oohed" and "ahhed" over my latest photos.

I knew, even without seeing what was attacking them, that my family all had their own issues, just like I did. I forgave them and I forgave myself, and we all had a peaceful Christmas Day. My gray sweatpants didn't look festive, but they had pockets that let me keep my phone nearby. I didn't need to keep looking at it, though. My gut told me I would see Shay soon.

26

One Step at a Time

The day after Christmas was a weekday, so I made some phone calls early. I looked up the ambulance company used to take Rose to Jon's. Charlie the paramedic couldn't talk about Rose, but he was able to give me the lowdown on Jon, since he wasn't a patient—yet. He was looking at a buffet of criminal charges, but might be able to plead insanity.

I spoke to Pastor Garrett at Shay's church. He said the doctors wouldn't immediately discharge Rose, but they agreed her sudden progress was nothing short of miraculous. Rose's family visited on Christmas Day, and Shay, Dylan, and the Justins had gone too. I asked the pastor for a favor. I grabbed my car keys and promised to follow my gut all day.

***

I rolled my car to a stop and parked. Maybe it was too early; I didn't see him. I got out and hunted around, saying hello to the homeless men who drifted by. Then I saw a familiar plaid coat on a man sitting on a milk crate. His head was almost down to his knees.

It didn't take much convincing to get him in my car. I guess when you live on the street, it hones whatever innate ability you may have to recognize good or evil. Not that people tend to find me threatening, but what is inside people can surprise you.

Major didn't know I was taking him to a job interview. I didn't want him to have a chance to get nervous. I parked at the front of the church and led him to the office. Pastor Garrett greeted him warmly, and they began chatting, the pastor's voice scratchy from the multiple Christmas services. After a while, Pastor Garrett thanked me and said I could go—meaning Major didn't need a ride back. I hovered a bit; I wasn't used to the idea that other people could manage to do things without me, but I was learning. I turned on the sight before I left. Major's demon seemed to be in agony. It wouldn't leave him without a struggle, but Major was a fighter.

***

After that, I drove my car without knowing where I was going. Maybe it didn't matter where I went—maybe he would find me. I smiled at that.

The mall was busy, but it was a low-key, grumpy sort of energy—not the pre-Christmas fervor. I strolled through the mall and picked the store that I thought would have the longest line of customers unhappy with their gifts. It was across from the vacant wreck of the Santa Land area. He wasn't in sight though—Shay, not Santa. If Shay were here, he would make these people laugh, make them feel better about themselves and each other. I could follow his lead on that kind of stuff, but I didn't know how to just go up and talk to strangers about personal things.

However, I did know how to take one step forward. And I knew that if I took that step forward for God, then a hundred angels would be right there with me. I took one step toward the line, then another.

I picked a woebegone man in the middle of the line and smiled at him, holding eye contact so he would know yes, I was smiling at him. "Wrong size or wrong gift?" I asked.

His eyes brightened, but for the wrong reason. "Do you work here?"

"No, I uh . . . I just . . ."

"She's just looking for that purple plaid Snuggie she didn't get for Christmas," said a voice behind me. "Now, now, you can't go mugging people in line." My heart swelled at the sound. A few people chuckled.

"You have the purple Snuggie?" I reached for the man's shopping bag like I was desperate. Shay pulled me back by my coat sleeve and turned me around for a hug. We swayed like we were dancing, then he exaggerated it till he was rocking me like a rag doll. People were laughing now.

His face had about 95 percent of its former carefree beam. Holding his face to pull it close, I said, "Rose is free now, and I thought you wanted to be with her. I love you, no matter how you feel about me. I know I will be fine."

Shay laughed and hugged me to his chest again. "Oh, El, I love you. I do feel an obligation to Rose." He pulled back to look at my face. "But it's the same obligation I feel to every living person on this Earth—to help them if I can. You, I love like the springtime and birdsong." He ran a hand through my hair, and it stuck in the tangles. "You just need to keep opening up so the sunlight can get in there."

I was happy to just stare into his eyes, but it would get awkward if I didn't say anything. "Um, you want to see a movie or something? *The Meaning of Christmas* is still showing."

He looked like he wasn't sure if I was joking, then leaned his forehead down to touch mine. "We can write our own story, El, and we don't need anyone else to tell us what it means. Let's go."

I nodded as he pulled back. *Later, I'll kiss him, but for now, we have things to do.* We intertwined our fingers as we walked along the line of weary shoppers, chatting with them and making them smile.

Acknowledgements

Two disclaimers to start with: First, despite Eliana's experience in this book, I am very much in favor of therapy. Second, I tried to make it clear in the story that what Eliana had was not really a seizure, but seemed enough like it that the emergency room doctors would not explore further.

My most heartfelt thanks go out to the more prominent members of the village that helped raise this book-child. I am grateful to my family and friends who have been as excited as I am about this novel. My critique group: Pat Daily, Lauran Kerr-Heraly, and Alex Perry, who motivated, encouraged and guided me. The now defunct Austin Screenwriters Group, whose meetings taught me story and technique, both from workshops and by example - I'm especially grateful to Nancy Smith and Wendy Wheeler. Wendy also designed the cover; more thanks! The members of the Brainstorming Group, especially Jessica Trapp for repeatedly creating communities for fellow writers. Thanks to Courtney Andersson of Elevation Editorial, for doing a thorough and excellent job of editing! Most of all, thank you to my husband, Ranjan, for the loving support and encouragement.

Amani Jesu writes about women finding the courage to be who they really are, often drawing on her own adventures in belly dance, photography, travel, and volunteerism. On one of her adventures she met her husband and love of her life in Nepal, the other side of the world from where they now live, in Houston, Texas.